The Greenacres Affair

Ian Searle

Copyright © 2022 Ian Searle

All rights reserved. No part of this publication may be reproduced or transmitted in any form or by any means, electronic or mechanical including photocopying, recording or any information storage or retrieval system, without prior permission in writing from the publishers.

The right of Ian Searle to be identified as the author of this work has been asserted by him in accordance with the Copyright, Designs and Patents Act 1988

First published in the United Kingdom in 2022 by
The Cloister House Press

ISBN 978-1-913460-56-3

Chapter one

Gordon left the little flat and made his way downstairs to begin his morning run. It was a ritual which he had performed for as long as he could remember. What he most liked about it was the opportunity to forget everything except his immediate environment. He was aware of the pounding of his feet, his breathing, the pace at which he was running, the fresh air he breathed and the hedgerows, wildflowers and farm animals who looked up with large, trusting, brown eyes as he passed. But things had changed. Ever since Sandra had broken the news, the very day that he was celebrating his degree, things were now different.

1960, he could not stop himself thinking, was proving an extraordinary year. He was young, and, until that moment, carefree. Two days after his graduation he had joined the university cricket eleven on their tour of England. He was looking forward to that – or had been.

"I'm pregnant," she said.

Gordon gaped in shocked disbelief. "Pregnant! Are you sure?"

"Of course, I'm sure."

"And it's mine?"

"What the hell are you suggesting? Of course, it's yours!"

Gordon had been so shocked that he was literally speechless. He opened and closed his mouth once or twice, then turned and walked out. Now, weeks later, he was consumed by guilt.

It was guilt which grew and intruded on every part of the day when he had a moment to reflect, as now, on his morning run. He was thoroughly ashamed of his behaviour, not for fathering a child, although that was a mistake, but in the way he had simply run away. At first, he was too confused to contact Sandra, then, as days turned into weeks, remorse made it harder to contact her and to try to sort out the mess. His friends on the cricket team noticed his change. He was abstracted, and not performing to his usual standard. That distressed him even further, but he did not feel able to tell anyone the cause.

He had never run this way before. He had moved into his little flat the previous day and realised that at the other side of the playing field there was a path by the river. It seemed a good place to explore. At any other time, it would have been invigorating and enjoyable. He had accepted the job as sports master only yesterday morning. Memories of the interview were fresh.

"Please sit down, Mr Drake" said the thin man, the older of the two. Gordon did as he was asked, facing the speaker and a second, slightly younger man. They were oddly complementary, the younger man, probably in his forties, had broad shoulders tapering down to his hips, which were concealed behind the table. He had the typical shape of a rugby league player. His older colleague was more like a pencil.

"My name is Harold Black," said the thin man, "I am the Deputy Headmaster, at the moment I am Acting Headmaster. My colleague is Raymond Carpenter, who has been in charge of our sporting activities, but is now obliged to step down."

"My interest is mainly in team games, especially rugby," said the younger man. "I would still like to be involved, but an old injury from my rugby league days compels me to step down."

"The situation at Greenacres," said Harold Black, "is unusual at present, which is why we are conducting this interview and why the post was not advertised earlier. As well as Mr Carpenter's having to step down on doctor's orders, we are currently without a headmaster. Our Headmaster, Mr Turvey, suffered a heart attack on the last day of term."

Gordon thought to himself the circumstances certainly were unusual, but they gave him an opportunity. He had been so preoccupied since he graduated in May, that he had failed to look for a full-time job until most of the teaching posts were already filled.

"Looking at your CV," said Raymond Carpenter, "I see your major interests and accomplishments are in track and field events and cricket."

"Yes," said Gordon. "I have spent the summer touring with the University Eleven, which is why I missed applying for the post earlier."

"What would you like to do if you got this job?"

"I assume the main sport during the winter is rugby?"

"At the moment, yes."

"Well, obviously, I would expect to continue that way, but it would be good to introduce some variety. I would like to see individual activities made available, if possible, as well as team games."

Raymond Carpenter nodded. "Sounds good," he said. "What activities have you in mind?"

"Some are obvious, I suppose, like cross-country. I don't know about equipment, but I should like to see a controlled programme of say, weight training. I'd like to think we could offer unusual things like shooting. I don't suppose there's enough space for a nine-hole golf course? You have a river here: could we perhaps introduce rowing, or at least sculling?"

"Whoa!" This time it was Harold Black. "These things could be very expensive, could they not?"

"Maybe," Gordon agreed, "but second-hand equipment might be available, and there are probably organisations, even businesses who might be approached as sponsors."

It was a strange interview, one for which Gordon could not prepare. He felt he was bluffing his way through. It lasted half an hour, and then he was asked to wait outside while they talked to each other. He sat on a simple chair in a large hall, the main entrance hall. The interview had been conducted in a room marked "Deputy Headmaster". A little further along was the Headmaster's Office. Windows in both these rooms gave onto the side of the building. The school office overlooked the front.

The façade was designed to impress, a neoclassical building, the main entrance framed by columns. From the entrance hall a grand staircase led up to the first- floor landing. Although the woodwork was waxed and polished, it was far from perfect and was marred by scuff marks. Gordon had noticed, when he climbed the short flight of steps to the front door, that the outside of the building looked a little run down. There were a few weeds sprouting at the edges of the steps, and the would-be splendid front door needed a new coat of paint.

The office door opened, and Harold Black called him back inside. "We are agreed," he said. "We should like to offer you the post of sports master, subject to references, of course. Mr Carpenter will show you round the school. You can make up your mind after that. We both hope you will accept."

Raymond Carpenter stood up. Gordon realised that he was walking with the aid of a stick. The "old injury" was clearly to his left leg. He limped quite heavily. Harold Black remained in his office as Carpenter began the tour. Gordon's initial impression of slight shabbiness was reinforced. As he was shown classrooms and other communal areas, the bottoms of the doors bore the marks of countless kicks. The paintwork throughout was also badly worn.

Carpenter led him down a long corridor on one side of which was the dining room and the kitchen, all stainless steel and professional. At the end of the corridor a door led into an open space. Gordon was impressed by the sheer scale of what was in front of him. Buildings had turned the flat space behind the original mansion into a quadrangle. At right angles to the main building were the dormitories, toilets, and washrooms for the 200 or so boys. At the far side of the quadrangle, parallel to the main building, were workshops and practical spaces for art, pottery, and a fully equipped mechanical engineering plant. There was even an old car on the far side of the workshops, covered in waterproof tarpaulin, it was used, said Carpenter, for the boys to dismantle and rebuild. It was in working order.

"Most of the sports equipment," Carpenter explained, "is stored in the groundsman's hut. That's down near the river."

"What about flooding?"

"We've never had a problem like that so far." He took the lead across the grass. It had not been cut for some time and, as Gordon had noted, the grass at the front of the school was in a similar state. It gave a poor impression. The groundsman's hut was screened from the rest of the buildings by a row of small trees. It was, Gordon thought, more like a barn than a hut. Carpenter produced a key with which he undid a large padlock. Gordon gave him a hand to open one of the big doors which were almost sealed by grass which had grown at their base. The "hut" was like Aladdin's cave, full of equipment of all kinds, including a small tractor and ganged mowers. He noted a stack of hurdles and similar equipment, all looking in need of repair or, at the very least, a coat of paint.

"What happened to the groundsman?" he asked.

"I'm not quite sure why," Carpenter replied, "but he left very suddenly a week before the end of term. A week later, poor old Turvey died of a heart attack. When Harold said it was a bit extraordinary, he was not joking."

They concluded their tour and Raymond Carpenter led the way back to the Deputy Headmaster's study.

Harold Black looked up from his desk. His face had a naturally dejected appearance, as though he were perpetually worried about something, but this time he really did look anxious.

"Well," he said, gesturing to Gordon to sit down again, "before you tell us your decision, I'd better give you the latest complication."

Raymond Carpenter looked quizzically at his colleague.

"The Governors in their wisdom," said Harold, "want the entire staff to report for duty ten days before term begins! It seems they have appointed a new Headmaster and he wants to speak to everybody individually. He seemingly wants to make some radical changes. It all sounds very mysterious and worrying. I just hope we can contact everybody. I imagine Irma – that's the School Secretary – will have forwarding addresses for some of them. This is all very irregular."

Raymond Carpenter was obviously surprised by this announcement. Gordon was merely baffled.

"I think I'd like to take the job," he said tentatively.

"Oh good! That's good," Harold said, but he was obviously distracted. "If you make your way to the School Office, and confirm your decision to the School Secretary, her husband, Frank, shares the office. He is the school Bursar. He will deal with your expenses and go through the standard contract. I'm sorry that we are all at sixes and sevens at the moment. And don't forget you will be expected to arrive for this preliminary meeting with the new Headmaster. That will be on Sunday, September 4, but everybody is expected to report in on Saturday, September 3. Term is due to begin on September 12."

The path was excellent for running, flat and not too winding. Gordon ran steadily for more than a mile when he came to a small bridge. The path continued the other side in both directions. He stepped onto the bridge and rested his hands on the wooden railing to stare down at the clear water. Patches of green weed grew at the bottom, waving in the current, and he could see fish flirting with the weeds. It was at that moment that he made up his mind; he would phone Sandra that evening. There was no phone in the flat. He had noticed a payphone in the entrance hall to the school, but he was reluctant to use that for such a personal call. He would go to the village – it was less than a mile from the school – and use the phone box there. He had no illusions about the reaction he could expect. Sandra would have every reason to be furious with him. He had behaved shamefully, like a rat and a coward. It was not fatherhood per se that so disturbed him as much as the way in which it would restrict his choices for the future. He did not want to marry Sandra, that much was certain, even if she tried to shame him into "doing the right thing". It would not work. He knew it, and Sandra probably knew it just as well.

He made his way back to the school buildings, showered, changed, and made himself a simple breakfast. He was not very hungry, and he knew he would not be hungry until he had made the phone call. He just hoped it would end the uncertainty and at least some of the guilt which he had been carrying for the past ten weeks. In that time, no doubt, pregnancy would have changed Sandra's life already. He had tried not to think about it, but now that the decision was taken, he had never in his life felt so nervous. All the guilt of the past weeks seemed to pile up like debris in a river, forming a dam which blocked his normal emotional existence. The phone call would release the pressure, but it would, he knew, be very painful. He had no excuses for his behaviour, and he was completely in the wrong.

He had no idea how he spent the rest of the day, but with a pocket full of coins in anticipation of a longish call, he walked the short distance to the village. The phone box was empty. He had half hoped, even now, that it would be occupied. He pulled open the heavy door, prepared some coins, and dialled Sandra's number.

His finger was trembling, and he wished he had a drink. It was Sandra's mother that answered the phone. He announced himself. She said nothing to him but called her daughter. He could not interpret her mood.

"So, you have finally decided to get in touch!"

"I'm sorry," he said. "I needed time to think."

"And you didn't bother to contact me before now?"

"No, I'm sorry, it is a bit of a mess."

"Yes, it is."

"That's not exactly what I meant," he said. "It's a mess here as well."

"Where are you anyway?"

"It's a private school in Sussex, a place called Greenacres."

"What kind of mess can you get into there? Not another girl?"

"No, nothing like that."

"Well, whatever it is, it can't be as important as fathering a baby. I knew you liked running. It never occurred to me that you would run so far and so fast."

"I know. I can only say I'm really sorry."

"So, what do you intend to do about it?"

"That's why I wanted to phone you."

"You've taken your time!"

"I know, I know. I just wanted to try to get things straight with you."

"It's a bit late for that! You get me pregnant and then run away! What kind of coward are you?"

"You have every right to be angry…"

"I have every right to be angry? How kind of you to say so," she said with heavy sarcasm. "Too bloody right, I'm angry. I'm the one carrying your child. You're the one running away from the responsibility. I can't run."

"I haven't got much money," Gordon was trying to find words to say what he had intended.

"Money? What the hell has money got to do with it? Do you think money would fix the problem? The problem is that I am going to be an unmarried mother."

"Unmarried?"

"Even if you asked me, do you think I would for a moment consider marrying a rat like you? At the first sign of a problem, all you can do is run as fast as your miserable little legs can take you. I wouldn't marry you if you were the last man on earth, though I'm not sure man is the right word. You are a contemptible worm!"

This was not entirely unexpected, nor, if he were honest, was it undeserved. He was at least relieved that Sandra had no more wish to marry him than he had to marry her.

"Give me your address," she said. "I don't want to talk to you or see you, but we have made a child between us. I shall look after it and probably love it, but I shall love it for itself, not because it is anything to do with you. On the other hand, I don't see why you should get away scot- free. I shall expect you to help with the expense."

Gordon gave her the address of the school.

"I told you there was a mess here. There is a new headmaster who says he will be making a lot of changes. I may not have this job for very long," he said.

"Then you had better find something else quickly. I shall need money for things like a pram, a cot, clothing, nappies and so on. I'll need maternity clothes for myself. I'm already beginning to show. I don't intend to put my own health at risk, working for nine months. I'll put all this in a letter. If you don't go along with it, I'll get a solicitor to help."

Gordon put down the phone. He felt more miserable than ever. Sandra had right on her side. She had only said what he had thought himself. He was relieved that she had no intention of pushing him into marriage, but he was worried about her threat to demand money from him without specifying how much.

On the other side of the road was a small, village pub. Gordon was not much of a drinker. He always said he had too much respect for his own body to abuse it with alcohol, but he did not want to go back to his flat to sit and brood. He went into the pub.

The public bar was empty except for one customer who sat at the counter. As Gordon sat on the next stool, the bartender appeared from another room.

"What can I get you?" he asked.

"A pint of bitter," Gordon ordered, "and I think I'll have a Scotch chaser."

The bartender drew the pint and put it in front of him, then turned to draw the whisky from an optic. "Just passing through?" he asked. "I haven't seen you here before."

"No, I just moved into Greenacres School."

At this the other customer looked interested. "What are you going to do there?" he asked.

"Take charge of sports."

"Ah! Carpenter's giving up at last, is he?"

"You know Greenacres?"

"I'm Stephen Wilder, Head of Maths."

"How do you do?" They shook hands. Gordon looked at his new colleague. He guessed that Wilder was in his forties. He had untidy, black hair. He wore thick-rimmed glasses. His skin looked sallow, unhealthy. Gordon noted that as soon as Wilder emptied his glass, the bartender replaced it with a full one. He was clearly a regular.

"What made you take the job at Greenacres?" Wilder asked.

Gordon explained that he had been late in the day applying for jobs. He had been touring Britain, he explained, playing cricket.

"Well, I must admit that Greenacres does not have much of a reputation in any sport. Cricket doesn't seem to be prominent. I don't even know where the pitch is – is pitch the right word?"

"Well, yes," said Gordon. "There's usually a special area, called a table, and it is used for more than one pitch. It needs to recover after a game."

"Sounds like me," said Wilder. Gordon could think of nothing to reply to this. He could not imagine Wilder being fit enough to play any kind of game, and judging by the amount of alcohol he was consuming, that would include darts or even dominoes.

He left the pub and walked back to the school. The alcohol had gone to his head, and he was regretting it. He was still reluctant to return to his flat so early in the evening, and he spent a little while wandering around the school grounds, getting acquainted with them. His emotions were still confused. He had hoped that by facing his problem and accepting the blame which Sandra had heaped on him, that he would feel much better. It was true that he felt relief at the removal of a possible threat, but he felt his behaviour was something he would never view with anything other than shame. It had taken him far too long to contact Sandra. He realised that he had shown himself to be a coward, and that was very hard to accept.

There were one or two people about. Today was September 3. Tomorrow, the new Headmaster would be talking to everybody. Gordon visited the main entrance hall and found a blackboard and easel had been set up facing the door. On it, neatly typed, was a programme for the next day. There would be a meeting in the Assembly Room (obviously not this hall, then) at 11 am. The Chairman of the Governors, Sir Lionel Beckingham, would introduce the new Headmaster, a Mr Grenville Mulcaster. At twelve noon there would be a break for a buffet lunch in the entrance hall. Mr Mulcaster would speak to all Heads of Department and the domiciliary staff (matrons) after lunch. After that, he would be calling on members of staff individually. There was no explanation of the purpose of these interviews. Gordon assumed, since he was the most recently appointed, that he would probably be down on the list. A note at the bottom of the programme warned everybody to keep an eye on further announcements.

Gordon slept well and woke refreshed. He repeated the run he had made the previous day. At some point, he told himself, he would cross that little bridge and explore the path on the other side of the river. To the left, downstream, it soon ran into a small wood. That would be interesting. To the right it probably led to another village.

Memories of the telephone conversation with Sandra were still with him, together with a kind of hangover of shame, but the fact that he had finally made the call was positive. It did not make up for his cowardice. From now on he would be slightly hampered financially, having to provide maintenance for his unborn child. That might be cause for a little worry, especially until the amount had been agreed. He hoped that would not result in acrimonious wrangling or even arguments with solicitors.

Just after half past ten he made his way back to the entrance hall. It was full of people, of whom he recognised only two or three. Harold Black, looking anxious, was nearby.

"Ah, Black!" A short, balding man with a powerful voice addressed the Deputy Headmaster.

"Sir Lionel," Harold Black replied, waiting to hear what the Chairman wanted.

"I've just realised," said the Chairman, "we did not mention your application for the headship. I'm sorry about that. Perhaps you are due an explanation."

"The appointment was for the governors to make," said Harold tamely.

"Yes, yes, yes. The fact is, Mulcaster seems to be exactly the right man for this job. You realise the school is in trouble?"

"Trouble? In what sense, Sir Lionel?"

"Numbers have been declining over the past two years. The curriculum that we offer has not changed in decades. The establishment of the new Comprehensive School just five miles away is offering a severe challenge. It can provide many of the programmes which we thought were unique. Being new, it has lots of money, and, for the parents it is free. Unless we make some radical changes, the odds are that we shall be out of business within a year. It's a huge challenge. Mulcaster may just pull it off, but, between you and me, it's going to be painful. We need to up our game, provide more academic success. Don't spread this around, but I fear there could be a number of staff redundancies."

Gordon was unashamedly eavesdropping on the conversation, and Sir Lionel's advice to keep it to himself was pointless, given the loud voice. The teachers – and there were about ten or twelve women, wearing white coats-overalls, matrons – were, for the most part, unsure of the purpose of this meeting. Many were indignant. They argued that changes could be introduced gradually, once the new headmaster had settled in. It would not be possible to make big changes and put them into operation within a week. Most were speculating on the kind of change this new man had in mind. Gordon caught the name Mulcaster and he inched his way a little closer to a group of three men.

"Frankly," said one of them, a man about fifty years old, grey-haired, intensely serious, "the man is simply a bastard."

"How exactly?"

"Good friends of mine sent their son to Merryman School. He was badly bullied. They took it up with Mulcaster, but he told them it was all part of growing up and the boy should learn to stick up for himself. Eventually, they withdrew the boy, but he told them bullying was rife. Shortly after that a fourteen-year-old took his own life."

"You're blaming Mulcaster?"

"The man is a bully himself. You'll soon find out. He gets results, but his methods are fifty years out of date. I think he probably models himself on Doctor Arnold."

"Doctor Arnold?"

"Head of Rugby School in the early days," the third member of the group explained. "The story goes that one boy was sent to him for not saying the Creed during morning prayers. When the boy explained that he did not believe in God, Arnold said,' you will believe in God by 4 o'clock this afternoon, or I shall beat you until you do!'"

This did not bode well for the future, Gordon thought, as he realised the noise was subsiding and the crowd was thinning. People were making their way to the Assembly Room. He followed suit. By the time he arrived the back three rows were already full. It always amused Gordon that people chose to sit at the back if they could. He sat at the end of a row, halfway from the front. Here, the noise was a little less, but there was still a great deal of conversation. After all, these were colleagues who knew each other and who had shared experiences in this building. They also were all wondering how the change of headmaster was going to affect them.

The large, wall clock showed exactly 11 am when the double doors opened to admit four people. Gordon was mildly surprised when everyone stood. One of the four was Harold Black, another was Frank Beauchamp, School Bursar, the third, Sir Lionel Beckingham. All eyes were on the fourth, a big man with a determined expression on a worn face. He stared at the audience. All except the Deputy Head sat down and the assembled staff followed suit. It was all at once silent.

"Colleagues," Harold began, "thank you for cutting short your holidays to attend this meeting. I'm sure you will understand why the Governors have taken this step, once everything has been explained.

"I would like to welcome Sir Lionel himself, as well as our new Headmaster, Mr Grenville Mulcaster. Mr Mulcaster began his teaching career as an assistant teacher in London, but teaching was not his original choice of profession. For three years he worked in banking. He is a fully qualified accountant. He began teaching Maths. He progressed rapidly and was made an adviser. Over the years his experience, enthusiasm and skill have meant he was consulted at the highest levels and acquired a reputation as a trouble-shooter. Several schools which were performing badly were rescued and are now thriving, thanks to his enthusiasm. We are fortunate to have him. I'm sure he will be a worthy successor to Mr Turvey."

The man sitting next to Gordon said quietly, under cover of the polite applause which followed, "Bit over the top, don't you think?" He spoke to his neighbour on the other side.

"Old Harold's buttering him up," came the whispered reply. "Probably worried about his job."

Sir Lionel stood up, apparently with pain.

"Thank you, Mr Black," he said. "I shall not say a great deal, because I think you will be concerned with what your new Headmaster has in mind. We are aware it may not be welcome to everyone." At this there was an audible murmur of doubt. "Let me say only this. The school finances are problematic. Enrolments have declined steadily for the past two years with the opening of the new Comprehensive School so close. Unless we can boost numbers, the Governors are seriously worried about the sustainability of the school. And to attract more pupils we need to make the school more successful. That is Mr Mulcaster's speciality, and we have told him we shall back him to the hilt, whatever he decides. As for me, I am now leaving Mr Mulcaster the floor. I leave you in his hands."

With that he walked with a noticeable limp to the door. His departure caught everyone by surprise.

Mr Mulcaster rose to his feet and pushed back his chair. He moved from behind the table to take his place in front. It was calculated to suggest he was speaking more directly to the assembled staff, discarding the protective barrier. There was something about his face that drew one's eyes. He was clean-shaven but his face, as Gordon described it to himself, looked lived in. His mouth was firm but mobile, though he remained serious throughout. His eyes were piercing. He held himself like a soldier, but he moved, despite his impressive stature, like a dancer, sure-footed, decisive.

"Ladies and gentlemen," he began, "as from tomorrow, I am officially a pensioner. But in a phone call, your chairman asked me to help sort out Greenacres School after the sad death of your last Headmaster. I have known Sir Lionel for many years. We have served together on several consultative committees. He explained the situation and painted a worrying picture of a school in decline. I was in London, so I asked for information to be sent to me. It was, indeed, worrying. You, who work here, must have at least an inkling. For the past three years the school, which is a charitable trust, has been losing money. The main reason seems to have been the decline in numbers. The tipping point was reached two years ago and, not to make too fine a point of it, unless drastic action is taken, by next year the Board may be forced to put the business into administration."

There was immediate, spontaneous reaction in the audience.

"I am not here to sweet-talk you," Mulcaster continued. "I am here with two things in mind. The first is to suggest what is and has been going wrong. The second is to recommend steps to remedy the situation. You will not like the conclusions I have reached on either count. The alternative, as I have said, could see the closure of Greenacres School within a year."

Even Gordon found this chilling.

"I have considerable experience," Mulcaster continued, "rescuing failing schools, which is why Sir Lionel called me in. I have formulated the beginnings of a plan, but, with the autumn term due to begin in a matter of days, many of the reforms cannot be introduced immediately. The Deputy Head, at my request, is drawing up a timetable which is similar to last year's. I hope the more radical reforms will be in place by January, though some must begin earlier. I am referring in particular to the examination classes. The results for 16- and 18-year-olds for the past three years have been frankly unacceptable. Key departments have been failing."

There were one or two protests at this, Mulcaster ignored them. Gordon thought he could also see one or two nods of approval.

"What seems apparent to me is a general air of neglect, maybe even apathy. To a casual observer there are tell-tale signs of a lack of leadership and pride, and that may have spread to the teaching itself. I do not know any of you personally yet, but I intend to scrutinise every member of staff more critically than most of you have ever experienced, however many years' service you have.

"The buildings and the grounds are untidy, reinforcing my remarks about the lack of pride. Yet this venue could regain all the attractiveness of a private, country park. I am, by the way, aware that the groundsman left and has not been replaced.

"The school cannot continue to spend money on the present scale. There are two options, both of which will be unpopular. There is, however, no other choice. We must either reduce the number of employees, mostly teaching staff, or you can all agree to a ten percent reduction in your salary."

There were cries of 'No!' and 'What?', 'You can't do that!'. Mulcaster waited for the hubbub to subside, then, still without raising his voice, he continued.

"No action will be taken immediately, but these decisions must be taken and implemented after Christmas. I am now going to take over Classroom Number 3 so that I can speak to groups of you together. Later, I shall move to the Headmaster's Office for individual discussions.

" There will be a lunch break in the Entrance Hall, then I would like to see all Heads of Department for an hour. After lunch I want to speak to those of you who are Heads of Houses and all the matrons, all those, in fact, concerned with overseeing the boarding arrangements. For the rest of the day and tomorrow I want to speak to each of you individually.

"Thank you for listening. I know this will be unwelcome and unsettling. I am not here to make friends, however. I am here to save this school. Thank you. One last thing, will Mr

Carpenter and Mr Drake please wait for a moment, when everyone has gone?"

The noise level rose to a crescendo. There was a mixture of shock, anger, indignation, and anxiety. They had not foreseen the threat to their jobs. The prospect of a cut in salary was especially unacceptable to most. As for ways to improve exam results, what did he know, they asked, about the recalcitrance, surliness and downright laziness of the teenagers they had wished upon them?

Gordon and Raymond Carpenter approached the front of the room and sat at Mulcaster's invitation. Both had no idea why they had been singled out.

"I asked you to stay behind," he said, "because of your involvement in the games programme. As you know, we have no groundsman. I intend to investigate the availability and cost of local, landscaping firms to see if we can contract them to cut the grass at regular intervals. I'm quite sure it would be cheaper than employing a groundsman. There are two snags. We still need to mark out rugby pitches and so on, and the grass is in urgent need of a trim now. Could the two of you cope with those things? Some of the older boys could surely do some of the work?"

"Some of the lads could do the marking, I suppose," Carpenter replied. This was an unexpected request. "I feel I should point out that I'm giving up the more active role on doctor's orders. I'll happily supervise marking out pitches, maybe even get the older boys to erect goalposts, but I don't think they should do the grass cutting."

"I'm happy to do that," Gordon said. "There's a Ferguson tractor and grass-cutting equipment in the groundsman's hut."

"Good," Mulcaster said. "Thank you for helping out. I appreciate your co-operation."

And that was that.

Gordon's name was not on what was soon known as the "Wanted List" so, after lunch, he set to work with the tractor. He enjoyed it, although he was obliged to stop from time to time as grass jammed the blades. By 4 pm he had cut all the grass in front of the school. He was driving to the back, when a short, plump lady held up he hand to stop him.

"That's thirsty-looking work," she said.

"It's a bit dusty," Gordon admitted.

"Well," she said, "my name's Penny Hastings, Head Cook. If you turn that thing off for a minute, I'll bring you a cup of tea. Can't have you treading all the clippings through the school, but it's so much better, now it's cut."

Gordon turned the key. It was suddenly quiet. He could hear the birds. He waited for Mrs Hastings and stepped down to stretch his legs. He looked back over the grounds he had already cut and appreciated for the first time what a difference he had made. It was more like a lawn, less like a field. From the end of the drive, the building would doubtless look smarter and grander. Mulcaster had a point; the school would be more attractive, but perhaps smartening up the place would encourage the staff, cooks or teachers, to feel pride.

He drank his tea and ate cake, leaning against the tractor, before making a start at the rear of the buildings. There was too much for one afternoon. He cut a swathe from the west end of the main building as far as the river and the groundsman's hut before making his way through an archway next to the workshops. The noise of the engine and the clatter of the grasscutters echoed from the building of the quad, but twenty minutes' work smartened it up.

Then he put away the equipment and cleaned it before taking another shower.

The grass-cutting exercise, which he had enjoyed, brought unexpected consequences. Almost everyone he met in the next twenty-four hours, spoke to him, mostly to commend him, though a couple of the older teachers queried whether he should be undertaking manual labour. Was it not, they asked, doing someone else's work? However, Raymond Carpenter was appreciative and, when Gordon continued the following day, mowing the land where the pitches would be, he was full of praise. Now, Gordon said, was the time to stake out a cricket table. Raymond was keen to plan the pitches to leave an area in the middle for that purpose. Neither Gordon nor Raymond were to know their plans would be halted in catastrophic circumstances.

Before that calamity, however, Gordon went for his morning run early on Monday, September 5. His conscience, like an upset stomach, was taking time to settle. The conversation with Sandra was in the past, but he was still waiting for the ominous letter she had promised. He would do his best to make amends, but he knew that his conscience would never be entirely at ease.

He ran as far as the bridge and paused once more. It was a beautiful morning. He was aware of birdsong and of the whispering, gurgling water. He watched fish as they lay, half-hidden in the weeds, heads towards him as they faced the current. Another sound prompted him to look up. Someone was running towards the bridge from the other side. A young woman in a tracksuit emerged from behind the trees. She stopped when she reached the bridge, long enough to say, "Hallo!"

"Hallo," he said. "Another runner! That's unexpected."

"I run here every day," she said. "Aren't you the new man, the tractor driver?"

He laughed. "That's me," he said, "Gordon Drake. I'll be looking after sport."

"Beth Shepherd, Domestic Science."

"Domestic Science?"

"I've got used to the surprise," she said. "I don't know how much you know about the history of Greenacres."

"Not much."

"Then you probably don't know the founder was a baker, and he left instructions that the school should provide not only a general education, but also an element of training in various trades, including cooking."

"That can't be why there's a fully equipped garage workshop."

Beth laughed. "Well, in a sense it is," she said. "Originally the boys learned how to look after horses, including blacksmithing, and they built and maintained carriages. When cars came in, they modernised. But come on, I'll race you back before we cool off."

To Gordon's surprise she ran quickly, and he had to work hard to keep up. When they reached the bottom of the field near the groundsman's hut, she suddenly sprinted. He made an extra effort but was only a metre ahead at the end.

"Wow!" he gasped, head down, hands on knees. "You're good!"

"I belong to a decent athletic club," she smiled. "I compete in mid-distance events."

"You'll have to tell me where this club is. I need to keep in shape. And, if you run every day, maybe we should run together."

"OK," she said, "But I always take the same route. I combine the run with a visit to my old Gran. She is very independent, but I worry about her."

"Sounds all right to me, though it makes you sound like Little Red Riding Hood."

"I'm assuming you're not a wolf. Do I need to bring an axe?"

"No, you won't be in danger, I promise."

They agreed to meet the following day at 6.30 by the river.

Chapter two

Detective Chief Inspector Edward Blundell stared gloomily at the file in front of him. He had been staring at it for five minutes without opening it. It contained statements, photographs, and documentation relating to a series of unsolved burglaries which had taken place over the past eighteen months. Chief Inspector Blundell hated paperwork, especially routine paperwork. It was ironic that his unexpected promotion from detective inspector to detective chief inspector had led to an increase in time spent reading files like these. At last, he reached out a great paw and opened the file. As he did so, his telephone rang. He picked it up with relief.

"Ted", said Superintendent Chris Potter, "I've got a strange one for you here. Do you know Greenacres School?"

"Never been there," he replied. "Everybody knows the place, of course. Big building in its own grounds. Not much of a reputation as a school, I believe. What's going on there?"

"A murder, or a suspicious death. Victim is a man called Grenville Mulcaster. He had just taken over as the new headmaster. The previous one died suddenly of a heart attack in July."

"Two of them in six weeks? What's going on?"

"That's what you'll have to find out. Get over there as soon as you can, will you, Ted? I said it looks like a strange case. This Mulcaster chappie crashed his car as he was driving away from the school last night."

"So, it's an RTA, not murder?"

"That's the strange bit. The traffic team say the brake fluid had been drained, and that caused the crash. Mulcaster drove down from London two days ago without incident, and he stayed at the school overnight. It looks as though the tampering must have taken place there. Apparently, the staff had been called back ten days before term, because the new headmaster proposed making some drastic changes."

"I suppose the place will be swarming with kids."

"No, their term doesn't begin until next Monday."

"I thought the schools went back today?"

"State schools, yes. Greenacres is independent."

"That's something, I suppose. One rule for the rich, as usual."

He put down the receiver and left his office. Eight CID men and two women turned, wondering what he wanted. He lost no time in telling them. Detective Sergeant Rawlings and two detective constables would travel with him in his car.

It was 8:30 am. The roads were busy with parents, taking their children to school. Once out of town, however, there was little traffic and by 9 o'clock they reached the turning to Greenacres School.

A uniformed constable was standing at the entrance to the drive.

"The wreckage is just inside the grounds," he said. "You'll need to walk, sir."

It was a matter of twenty yards from the entrance. Mulcaster's car had failed to turn as the sloping drive neared the road. There were no skid marks, but the vehicle had careered into one of the trees that marked the edge of the estate.

"The body has been removed," the constable explained. "The surgeon reckoned death was instantaneous."

A policeman in a boiler suit was peering into the buckled remains of the engine compartment. He straightened up when The Bear approached. He wore sergeant's stripes.

"Not an accident?"

"No, sir. Someone had cut through the brake pipe with some kind of tin snips, probably."

"Wouldn't that be obvious? Surely the oil would make a puddle the driver could see?"

"Yes, sir, that's exactly right, unless whoever it was put something in place to collect the oil."

"Premeditated sabotage?"

"It has to be."

"And the poor sod wouldn't have known about it until the brakes failed?"

"No. The car was left at the back of the school for two nights. He would have left the handbrake on and had no reason to use the foot brake until he was slowing to take this bend."

"We need to get up to the school," said The Bear. "Can we drive past?"

"Sorry, sir, they're still measuring up and taking pictures. I'm afraid you'll have to walk."

The Bear growled, a sound expressing resignation, and then he called his three colleagues to walk with him to the building. He noted that the grass had been recently cut. The cuttings were beginning to dry out. The building looked like a stately home. The Bear felt mildly hostile; he disliked the privileges associated with inherited wealth. This imposing mansion had no place in the modern world.

A man and a woman watched from the top step as the four policemen approached. The woman wore a plain skirt and blouse. She was of indeterminate age. She wore very little makeup. Her hair was tidy, shoulder-length, dark, not stylish. The man beside her was much older, tall, but slightly bowed, he had grey hair. Like the woman, he wore glasses. Neither of them looked especially welcoming, but the man seemed anxious.

"Good morning," he said, when they were close enough. "Can we help you? My name is Black,

Acting Headmaster, and this is Mrs Beauchamp, School Secretary."

"DCI Blundell," The Bear introduced himself, briefly showing his warrant card. "Can we go inside somewhere?"

The Secretary opened the thick door and led the way into a large hall. The wide staircase, opposite the main door, drew the eye.

"Perhaps," suggested Mr Black, "we should use one of the classrooms since there are so many." He led the way to the right of the stairs into a tunnel-like corridor and opened a door. It was a small classroom. There were individual tables and fifteen chairs. The only similarity to classrooms The Bear remembered, was the blackboard They all sat down.

"Well, Inspector," Mr Black began.

"Chief Inspector," The Bear corrected him.

"I am intrigued to discover why you feel the need to bring so many colleagues to investigate a road accident."

"Normally," The Bear explained, "Traffic would be in charge, but this was not an accident."

Harold Black looked shocked. "You're surely not going to tell us Mr Mulcaster deliberately ran his car into a tree? Suicide?"

"No, not suicide."

"But if it isn't an accident nor suicide…"

The Bear nodded. "Right. We are certain someone tampered with the brakes to cause the crash."

The shock was deeper now.

"But" Harold Black was groping for an explanation," he drove the car all the way from London on Saturday."

"So we understand."

"So, was it just bad luck that the accident happened when it did?"

"Our forensic experts believe the damage must have been done while the car was here, at Greenacres School."

"Oh, dear God!" The implications were enormous.

"There is almost certainly someone here in your school who is responsible for Mr Mulcaster's death. We shall need to interview everyone who was here and who had access to the car. That means interviewing everyone. We shall need to establish everybody's whereabouts at all times."

Harold Black stared at the big man and seemed to wilt like a hothouse plant starved of water.

"Oh dear! Oh dear!" he muttered." This could be the nail in our coffin." He was looking at the School Secretary as he spoke. "The boys are due back this weekend."

"You may need to change that," said The Bear. "I can't guarantee we'll be finished by then, We shall need to search the area where the vehicle was kept."

"Postpone the term? The parents will find that very hard to cope with."

"We would have to contact parents of 200 children," the School Secretary was also shocked at the prospect.

"I must consult Sir Lionel," Harold Black said.

"Sir Lionel? The Bear sought clarification.

"Our Chairman of Governors."

"Right," said The Bear. "Mrs Beauchamp, while Mr Black does that, there are a number of things I want done. I want a complete list of all those who have been living in the school premises for the past three days. I shall also want them called together immediately, so I can explain to them what is going on. Sergeant Rawlings here will draw up lists and times for everyone to make statements. I shall occupy the dead man's office. I shall want you to help uncover as much information as possible about Mr Mulcaster. The area at the bottom of the drive is a crime scene, so no vehicles can enter or leave until the preliminary work is complete. I may need to bring in more men to carry out the investigation. Any questions?"

Irma Beauchamp and Harold Black were staring, open-mouthed.

"Oh, I did forget," The Bear added, "we tend to drink a lot of tea, if you could organise that."

The Bear's arrival at Greenacres School was like throwing a lighted cigarette end into a box of fireworks. The result was consternation and alarm. Irma Beauchamp and her husband had been accustomed for the past three years to running the routine affairs of the school. The previous headmaster had left almost everything to them to deal with. The governors saw no reason to interfere. So, when The Bear took charge abruptly, they were both disconcerted. Irma was unhappy at being told what to do by total stranger, but The Bear was a stranger with power. She had no option but to do as he asked. She took pride in doing it well, however, and this gave her a degree of comfort. So far, The Bear had made no demands on the Bursar.

Once settled in the Headmasters Study, The Bear lost no time, organising his forces by telephone. When Irma asked it if the police would pick up the bill for the phone calls, he replied testily, "Of course, you will just have to submit a claim." It looked like being a big one. The investigation at the bottom of the drive would not be complete before the evening at the earliest. That was a complication, but one which just had to be accepted. The Bear arrange for his team, consisting of a further six CID officers, to drive as far as the main entrance, and to walk from there. When Irma explained that the dead man had been appointed by the Governors, The Bear wanted to talk to the Chairman, Sir Lionel. Sir Lionel would find it very difficult to walk from the road up to the school, so, he was asked to drive as far as he could, and Frank Beauchamp was asked to drive down as far as the scene of the crash to collect him. Frank in his turn was unhappy at being treated like an unpaid driver, but he did as asked.

Sir Lionel, like the rest of the staff, was affronted by the police take over. Leaning heavily on his stick, he limped into the Study and sat. He was a small man but used to authority. The stare he gave The Bear was belligerent rather than cooperative.

"What kind of nonsense is this?" he asked.

"It's not nonsense," said The Bear. "A man has been killed. My job is to find out why and who killed him."

"I understood that Mulcaster lost control of his car and drove into the tree."

"Only partly true," said The Bear. "There is nothing to indicate this was a matter of driver error. Examination of the wreckage, however, reveals something far more sinister. Someone had deliberately tampered with the brakes."

"Good God! Why would anyone do that?"

That's what I'm here for. We need full cooperation from everybody in the school."

Sir Lionel was bemused. "Naturally," he said, "you will get that. When was this tampering done? Could it have been done before Mulcaster arrived at the school?"

"We have already ruled that out," The Bear explained, and he repeated his explanation that Mulcaster had driven all the way from London without incident. "While we shall be looking closely at where the car was parked, and who might have had access to it, I am also concerned with the motive which drove whoever it was to take this action. Mulcaster's car was readily identified as his, being both large and unlike any of the cars belonging to the residents. I think we can rule out that whoever did this might have mistaken the vehicle. I am personally sure it was a deliberate attempt – a successful attempt – on Mulcaster's life."

"Murder!" It was a thought which Sir Lionel had not allowed until this moment. "This is terrible! Among other things, it is likely to ruin the school."

"Not my concern," said The Bear, dismissing the idea has of no consequence. "I am interested in tracking down a dangerous criminal and putting him behind bars. I don't much care about your school, I'm afraid."

"Perhaps you can understand my position," said Sir Lionel. "We the Governors, are legally responsible for this school. It employs upwards of forty staff. We provide a specialised education for 200 children. Their parents have their own commitments and, if the school is obliged to close, they will not only have to make other arrangements for their children, they may be obliged to take time away from their own work. The consequences are widespread."

"I fully understand that," said The Bear. "As I said, however, all that is your problem, not mine. If I am to track down this man or woman – I suppose it could be either – I need to know why he or she was determined to kill or at least to injure Mr Mulcaster. Since he was appointed by the Governors, I hoped you could tell me a little bit about him."

"I did not know him very well personally," said Sir Lionel. "It was a colleague, another Governor, who recommended him. Mulcaster was on the point of retirement from Merryman school. He had an excellent record over the years, immediately to post-war, of rebuilding schools which had begun to fail. Greenacres was in a similar situation, suffering from competition with the newly built comprehensive in Markham. It is only five miles away."

"It's said 'since the war'. Was he teaching during the war, do you know?"

"No. I don't know if it was because his discipline was mathematics, but he was called up at the beginning of the war and served more than five years in the Intelligence Corps. More than that I do not know. We were really only interested in his work as a headmaster."

"Who was the colleague you referred to? The one who recommended him?"

"Vincent Walters."

"And how can I contact him?"

Sir Lionel fumbled in his pocket and took out a small pocketbook. He thumbed the pages, found the name he was looking for, and gave The Bear a telephone number. He warned him that Walters would probably not be available during the daytime, as he was retired and spent much of his time on the golf course. The Bear shifted in his seat as a sign of disapproval, but he thanked Sir Lionel.

"Is this investigation likely to interfere with the beginning of term?" Sir Lionel asked.

"That seems very likely. We have a lot of people to interview, and we shall need the forensic team on site for some time. I would suggest you postpone the beginning of term for at least two further weeks."

"I suspect," said Sir Lionel, "once the news gets out that this is more than a simple accident, it spells the end of the school. Parents won't want to send their boys here. This is a total disaster."

On that miserable note, he let himself out of the office to go and chat with Frank Beauchamp. Irma was frantically busy typing up lists. She may not enjoy the work in the circumstances, but she was determined to do it well.

School secretaries, it seemed, did not take the same holidays as the teaching staff. The Bear was able to speak the the Secretary at Merryman School. He explained there had been an accident and he needed information about Grenville Mulcaster. The Bear was interested in the response. The Secretary, Mrs Thompson, was not unduly shocked. She dealt with his questions politely but expressed no regrets that her former boss was dead. She promised to have Mulcaster's personal file ready for collection by a police officer.

"Tell me," The Bear said, once this was arranged, "what did you think of him personally?"

"He was my boss," she said.

"How did he treat you?"

She did not answer immediately, then, "He didn't like women much," she said. "He always seemed to talk down to me. I suppose he was a bit of a bully."

"But an efficient one?"

"Yes, you could say that. He was very good with figures. He probably saved us thousands, one way or another."

Under the watchful eye of Sergeant Rawlings the team had knocked on the door of every resident in the main school building. They were all asked a few important questions about their whereabouts during the evening and night of September 4th and 5th, when someone had tampered with the car, and they were told they would be required to make a formal statement. As well as the Headmaster's flat, at the front of the house on the first floor, the rest of the first and second floors had been converted into apartments. Most of these were occupied by teaching staff. Detective Constable Jones handed his written reports to Rawlings with an apology.

"Sorry, Sarge," he said, "I'm not sure of the spellings. I'm not used to Indian names."

"Indians? You'll be telling me there are cowboys after them."

"Not Red Indians," Jones replied, taking Rawlings joke at its face value, "Indians from India."

"Teachers?"

"Not as far as I could understand. The first of them was a woman. When she opened the door and saw the uniform, she was terrified. She slammed the door in my face. The next one was a man. He wasn't too keen to cooperate, either. I'm pretty sure there were several more in the two flats. The man spoke some English and gave me the names of the others."

"Sounds funny," said Rawlings, and he lost no time in passing the information to The Bear.

Irma Beauchamp was not pleased to be interrupted. Her voice on the phone was crisp. "We have three Punjabis on the staff," she explained. "They needed to escape because there has been unrest there ever since Partition. They are excellent workers. One of them helps in the kitchen, the other two are cleaners. You can't possibly think they had anything to do with Mr Mulcaster's death?"

"We can't rule anyone out yet," said The Bear, and replaced the receiver. There was something strange going on, all the same. He would probably want to interview these Indians personally.

For the moment, however, he was on the look-out for any resident who had a long-standing connection with Mulcaster. None of the staff had worked at Merryman School, but he suspected the private school world was a sort of subculture in which there were many hidden connections. There must be something in the past that would lead to Mulcaster's killer. It might take a long time to find it. The team had been alerted to look for connections.

It was, of course, possible that the motive did not date from the past, but Mulcaster may have overstepped the mark here in the first few hours. It seemed unlikely that he could generate such a strong reaction of hate in so short a time. He had said he was not out to make friends. He had offered an ultimatum; the staff could accept his plans or face redundancy. Was that enough to provoke violence? Whoever had tampered with the brakes on Mulcaster's car must have known it was his. It was a premeditated crime. Perhaps it would be sensible to probe more deeply into what had taken place in some of the individual interviews which Mulcastter had held. The Bear looked at the list of names which had been posted. The first name was Harold Black. He would begin there.

"Tell me what was said in the interview you had with Mulcaster,," he asked.

"What exactly do you want to know?"

"Did Mulcaster have plans for the school and the staff, involving you?"

"Naturally," said Black "He needed my knowledge and assistance as Deputy Headmaster. He had already spoken to me and asked me to draw up a timetable for the coning term."

"Yes, I know that" said The Bear impatiently. "What did he say about your position as Deputy Head? He planned to keep you on?"

"Keep me on? Of course. It was not in his power to do otherwise. The Governors appointed me."

"And the Governors told him they would go along with whatever he decided."

Harold Black stared at the Chief Inspector with distaste that turned into deep antagonism. "Where is this going?" he asked. "Mr Mulcaster had a difficult job to do. My job was to assist him. That is what I was going to do."

"Was he happy that you were the man for the job? Dis he, perhaps, hint that you might be replaced or even sacked at the end of term?"

The indignation on Harold Black's face was such that at any other time it would have seemed comical. "Absolutely not!" he spluttered. "Our discussion was polite, professional and mutually respectful. We discussed the need to weed out weaker members of staff, but the discussion was in total confidence and at no point was there a hint that my own position was at risk."

"Right." The Bear ignored the hostile tone. "I assume you would never consider yourself to be one of the weaker members of staff. For the moment I must assume Mulcaster felt the same way. What about the teachers you discussed?"

"What about them?"

"Can you name them?"

"You are asking me to discuss personal, highly confidential matters of opinion and professional judgement."

"Yes, I am."

The two men stared at each other in silence.

"I don't think I can report such matters to you," said the Deputy Head.

"You have no choice in the matter, Mr Black. This is a murder enquiry, and you are obliged by law to tell me what you know."

There was another silence.

"Very well," Black said at length. "What we tried to determine was the long-term future of the school. Mr Mulcaster proposed fundamental changes to the curriculum, but some of them would contradict the original foundation. He wanted to end some of the more practical courses, such as Domestic Science, perhaps Mechanical Engineering, and cut down on others, such as Art and Ceramics."

"And the teachers?"

"Some would lose their jobs; others could be reduced to part-time. But there was more to it than that. Most of the staff involved live in and would have to find alternative accommodation."

"Pretty drastic, then. Was Mulcaster proposing to put these plans to the staff involved?"

"So he told me, yes."

The Bear frowned. "What about the rest of the staff?" he asked. "You mentioned weak teachers."

Black looked distressed by the question. He took his time answering. "Well," he said at last, "Mr Mulcaster had two strings to his personal bow: he was a mathematician and a chartered accountant. He aimed to make the future Greenacres School cost-effective and acquire an excellent reputation for its standard of Mathematics."

"That suggests he was not satisfied with the Maths being taught."

Harold Black nodded reluctantly.

"Which teachers were threatened? More than one?"

Again, a reluctant nod. "We have three Maths teachers," he said, "the Head of Department is Stephen Wilder who has – personal problems.."

"What kind of personal problems?"

"He is still suffering from his experiences in the war?"

"He was injured, you mean?"

"Not exactly. He's a veteran of Dunkirk and of the D-Day landings."

"Him and thousands of others."

"That's as may be, but Stephen's experiences of both were very traumatic. He suffered a breakdown when he was released."

"That was fifteen years ago."

"The effects are still with him."

"What effects are you talking about?"

"He suffers from nightmares, that sort of thing."

"This affects his teaching?"

Black shifted uneasily. "This is really a matter for you to take up with him yourself rather than discuss behind his back."

"I shall do that, but it would help if you, as an experienced teacher yourself, could explain how Stephen Wilder's experiences fifteen years ago affect his work in the classroom."

Harold Black was squirming in his reluctance to be more specific. At last, he explained in a confidential voice that was almost a whisper. "The only way poor Stephen can cope," he said, "is to dull his senses with alcohol."

The Bear sat back in shocked surprise.

"A drunk? And this is common knowledge?"

"He can't altogether hide it, poor chap."

"From the pupils?"

"I – we think many of them realise. Some are puzzled, some seem to find it funny."

"What about the parents?"

"We have occasionally had to respond to complaints. That has fallen to me. Turvey, the previous Headmaster, handed complaints to me to deal with."

The Bear looked at him with a mixture of disbelief and pity. It sounded as if Wilder should have been sacked long ago, but Harold Black had certainly ended up with the dirty end of the stick. The Bear needed time to think about this before he interviewed the Head of Mathematics. Wilder would surely have been aware that Mulcaster was a mathematician, and he would have been anxious about his future. That and nightmares from the past would make him unstable in the extreme. He could speculate on the subject, but he needed to talk to Wilder.

Rather than stay in the Headmaster's Study and phone Sergeant Rawlings, The Bear stretched his legs.

"How's it going, S.ergeant?" he asked.

"We're getting there," Rawlngs replied. "Three more reports for you." He handed them over. "I'm still wondering what all these Punjabis are doing here. I know three of them are on the payroll, but there must be at least half a dozen others. Are they all legit, do you think?"

"Good question. Find out what you can, but we're first and foremost interested in alibis."

"Nobody seems to have one,," said Rawlings. "No one has so far seen anybody tampering with the car. This could take some time, Boss."

The Bear gave one of his growls. Rawlings looked down at the papers on the table to hide the grin the familiar sound provoked. One of his colleagues had once remarked it was the sort of sound you got when you turned a real teddy bear on its back. The image stuck. Rawlings had an instant picture of the DSI tipped on his back. But The Bear was on his way back to his own office.

He was reaching for the doorhandle when an imperious, female voice demanded, "Are you the man in charge?"

He turned round. The woman was almost statuesque, about five feet nine inches tall, dressed in a plain, but expensive dress. Her hair was carefully styled and probably coloured. It was the hair style of a younger woman. Her face was sharp-featured, with a prominent nose, narrow eyes which could not be made to look wider by the eyeshadow. The mouth was set in a firm line, a slash of purple lipstick. She was looking The Bear in the eye, demanding attention.

"I'm Detective Chief Inspector Blundell," he replied. "I'm in charge of this investigation. Who are you?"

"I'm Thelma Black. My husband is Acting Headmaster."

"I see. How do you do? What can I do for you?"

"I've come to complain."

"About what exactly? I am very busy. Perhaps you could speak to my Sergeant. He's in Classroom number three."

"I know where he is. It's you I want to speak to."

"Can you please make it quick, Mrs Black?"

"I object to being treated like a common criminal."

"I don't understand."

"One of your constables actually knocked on my door and demanded a statement."

"We are talking to everyone on the premises."

"But there is surely no need to treat senior staff like criminals!"

"I'm sorry you feel that way, but we have a job to do."

"You should show more respect."

"I'm sorry, I haven't got time to waste on this." The Bear turned back to the door.

"You have no right," Thelma said, her voice loud and peremptory, "to be using this office."

The Bear turned back, surprised.

"It's the Headmaster's Office," she continued. "My husband should be there. He's the Headmaster now."

"He may be the Acting Headmaster," said The Bear tersely, "but I'm in charge at the moment. I don't have time to waste on trivial matters."

Thelma Black was still remonstrating as he closed the door behind him. He caught an indignant, frustrated call of "Oh really!" He was suddenly reminded of the harsh call of a crow. He took his place behind the desk, thinking what a genuinely miserable life Harold Black must lead at home as well as at work.

He was not pleased when it proved difficult to track down Stephen Wilder. He filled some of the time by making a call to Sir Lionel.

"How and when was Stephen Wilder appointed?" he asked.

"Stephen? He was made Head of Mathematics ten years ago. Why do you ask?"

The Bear ignored the question. "What kind of procedure was used?"

"I don't understand."

"I assume the post was advertised and the candidates asked to give references?"

"Yes, but it was a little different in this case."

"In what way?"

"It has always been difficult to find Maths teachers. Stephen was the only applicant."

"Really? What about his referees?"

Sir Lionel did not reply for a moment.

"Sir Lionel?"

"Yes, I'm sorry. This will sound unusual, but I was the principal referee."

"You?"

"Stephen is my godson."

This was unexpected and it was The Bear's turn to think before replying. Then, "You are aware, I take it, that he has a drink problem?"

"It is not that simple. The poor fellow had a distinguished career in the army, but he was under terrible stress. When he was demobbed at last, it caught up with him and he suffered a nervous breakdown."

"That would surely not be the best condition to equip him to be a teacher?"

"Stephen is a fundamentally good man, intelligent, and good at Maths."

"But he drinks."

"It is his way of coping."

"Have there not been complaints?"

Sir Lionel took his time. "I must admit I have had to defend him from time to time. I paid for him to attend a private clinic twice. Each time it worked for a few months before he relapsed."

"Surely, he should have been sacked?"

"You must understand I have known Stephen all his life. His parents are both dead. I'm his only hope."

"What about your responsibility as a Governor?"

"I was torn. But on Saturday I gave him an ultimatum; I would pay for one more course of treatment. If he refused or took it up and gave up, I would ensure that he lost his job."

"Did he accept?"

"He was supposed to decide by today."

The Bear thought for a while. "You say he had this mental breakdown because of his war service," he said, "but thousands of men must have had the same experiences without breaking down."

"Perhaps I've made him sound weak," said Sir Lionel, "But it was one incident towards the end of the war that was the trigger. Stephen was in command of a handful of men and was ordered to capture a building on the outskirts of Caen. Intelligence in the UK, built on aerial photographs indicated the surrounding area was clear. It was wrong. Stephen was the only survivor. He saw eleven friends shot to pieces literally. It was carnage."

The Bear felt more sympathetic, but, as he replaced the receiver, he remained convinced Stephen Wilder should never have been appointed to teach. He could scarcely be more unsuitable. It would be interesting, when he eventually turned up for an interview, to assess how unstable he was. If he was not weak, as his godfather said, was he simply unpredictable? Mulcaster was a mathematician who would almost certainly have sacked Wilder. Was that a motive to tamper with the brakes?

"You wanted to speak to me?" Stephen Wilder came in and sat down opposite The Bear.

"Yes, and I did ask everybody to stay within call. We have had trouble trying to find you."

"Sorry" He did not sound contrite. "I didn't imagine you would want to speak to me, since I had nothing to do with Mulcastor's death. I have to admit I'm not exactly sorry."

"That sounds very hard thing to say. What had you against the man?"

"His bungling ruined my life."

"What on earth makes you say that?"

"I had a bloody awful war, one way or another."

"What has that to do with Mulcaster?"

He was responsible for the deaths of eleven of my friends and comrades."

"Mulcaster? How come? As I understand it, he spent the entire war in this country."

"Too bloody right! He was one of those who led from behind."

"He was in the Intelligence Corps."

"That's right. No face to face fighting for him. He was safe at home."

"So, why do you say he was responsible for the deaths of your comrades?"

"I only found out later, when I was sent back home to hospital."

"Exactly what did you find out?"

"Twelve of us were ordered to take over a house on the outskirts of Caen. It would be simple, we were told. Reconnaissance reported it was undefended. There were two heavy machine gun emplacements. They took us completely unprepared. I survived. The others all died. I was so angry that I asked a lot of questions and eventually tracked down the man who had given us the wrong information, a Major Mulcaster." Wilder stubbed out a cigarette after lighting another from the stub. His hands were shaking, and, from the other side of the desk, The Bear caught a whiff of alcohol.

"So, you had a long-standing grudge..?"

"Grudge! It was a bloody sight more than a grudge! I hated the man."

The Bear stared at the sallow face with its red-rimmed eyes. "You realise what you are saying?" he asked.

"You mean I'm a suspect? Do you think I care? I didn't tamper with his car, but, if I had, I'd be proud of it."

"I think," said The Bear, "you've been drinking. I shall want to interview you again when you are sober. You might otherwise deny what you have said so far. You are certainly a suspect, so, go away and sober up. Don't go away too far this time."

Wilder stood up, pushing the chair aside clumsily and took three slightly uncertain steps to the door.

The Bear stared after him. Wilder was a prime suspect, but there was no hard evidence as yet. Was it alcohol that prompted him to speak as he did? Wilder was the only resident so far who had admitted to knowing Mulcaster before his appointment. Sir Lionel knew him, but he did not live in the school. Was the Governor aware of the connection between Mulcaster and his godson? Could he be complicit with Wilder? But these questions were no more than creative guesswork without further evidence.

If Mulcaster had been seriously considering the closure of some departments, there were several teachers with every reason to stop him. Harold Black had mentioned Maths as likely to be remodelled, but had mentioned two Heads of Department who could lose their jobs, Home Economics and Car Mechanics. Considering the way in which the death had been planned, someone who was familiar with cars was worth talking to. The Mechanical Workshops teacher was a Clifford Jackson. The Home Economics teacher was a woman called Beth Shepherd. On first sight it would seem less likely that she would commit such a crime. Both would have to be interviewed.

The main problem was that anyone could have cut the brake pipes. Finding someone with a strong motive had so far brought up Wilder. Was it even credible that the threat of redundancy would be enough for one of the other teachers to take such drastic action? It was surely very unlikely, but it was an angle which The Bear felt he had to explore. The more unlikely candidate of the two was the Head of Domestic Science, the young woman called Beth Shepherd. He called for her first.

"According to your statement," he began, "you spent Monday evening in your flat."

"Yes."

"Were you alone?"

"I was, yes."

"Is there anyone who can confirm that you were in your flat for the entire evening?"

"I should hardly think so. I spent the evening on my own, as I said."

"No visitors?"

"No."

"Did you perhaps watch television? Can you tell me what programs you watched?"

"I didn't watch any television. I read a book."

"So, we have only your word for it that you didn't leave your flat."

"That's usually enough," said Beth, her feathers slightly ruffled.

"The circumstances aren't usual," The Bear pointed out. "We are talking about the evening that someone deliberately tampered with the brakes on Mr Mulcaster's car."

"I understand that" said Beth, "but it wasn't me. I had no reason to do such a thing."

"You are Head of Domestic Science, are you not?"

"Yes."

"I understand that your department was threatened with closure."

"That's what I understood, too."

"That would mean you lost your job!"

"If it happened, yes, but I'm far from sure that it would happen."

"Why not?"

"One of the things that gave Greenacres its special status was the foundation document. It dates back to the 1880s, I believe. The founder of the school stipulated that boys shall be taught basic, domestic skills. Many of them would end up in the forces, where they would often have to look after themselves. I happen to believe that it is just as important for boys as it is for girls to have skills such as cooking. Even looking after their own clothing is valuable."

"And if that tradition was to be overturned?"

"It would be sad and wrong."

"And a bit of a disaster for you, I imagine."

"The assumption behind what you are saying is absurd," said Beth, looking The Bear in the face, "I am well qualified. I would have no difficulty finding another job. It would be more than inconvenient, I must admit."

"Why more than inconvenient?"

"Greenacres is beautifully situated for me," said Beth. "I have a grandmother who lives a short distance away on the other side of the river. I visit her every morning to keep an eye on her. She has been unwell for some time, so this is very convenient. If I moved away, I would be quite worried about her welfare."

"You realise that you may find yourself looking for another job, anyway?"

"That worries me far more than your totally unjustified inference that I had something to do with Mr Mulcaster's death. Mr Black has already suggested to us that the school may be forced to close. I hadn't realised just how serious the financial situation was."

The Bear grunted. "Thank you, Miss Shepherd," he said. "Please stay within reach where we can find you, if we need to."

The door closed behind her, and The Bear stared at it for a moment. She seemed honest and he did not believe she had a plausible motive, even if she had the opportunity to tamper with the car. The kind of tampering in question did not need specialist knowledge. Most of these teachers were drivers and all of them had access to the maintenance facilities. The next person to be interviewed would certainly have the correct skills and he might also have far stronger feelings about the threat to his position. It was the Head of Mechanical Engineering.

Clifford Jackson was a presentable man in his thirties. He gave The Bear a belligerent stare and sat down.

"According to your statement," The Bear began," you spent Monday evening with a friend."

Jackson said nothing.

"Is that correct?"

"That's what I said," said Jackson.

"When did you get back?"

"Is that any of your business?"

"Yes, it is my business," said The Bear. "I'm conducting a murder investigation. I am not in the habit of asking unnecessary questions."

"I spent the night with her and got back some time before seven."

"Seven am?"

"Yes."

"Her name?"

"Jessie Walker."

"We shall need to speak to her."

"If you must." Jackson seemed unperturbed.

"Did you go near Mr Mulcaster's car on your way out or coming back?"

"No."

"In your job you are, I assume, familiar with most makes of car?"

"Pretty much, yes."

"Did you notice Mr Muncaster's car?"

"Yes, a two-litre Rover, a bit showy. It's what I would call all fur coat and no knickers."

"Did you have a good look at it?"

"Not especially. I saw it parked outside. I remember thinking it was a neat bit of parking in the corner."

"Close to your workshop?"

"Depends what you mean by close. About ten or fifteen yards away I suppose."

"Would it have been easy for anybody to tamper with it without being seen?"

"That would depend on when he did it. Whoever it was, he would be taking a chance in the daytime."

"After dark?"

"Still a bit of a risk, but he could have got between the car and the wall, I suppose."

"When this person cut the brake line, wouldn't the brake fluid have run out straightaway and left a puddle?"

"Yes, it would, unless he put something underneath to catch it."

"You must have done this sort of thing – bled the brakes – isn't that what you call it? –what do you use to catch the fluid?"

"I use a tray. There's not too much oil in the brake system. Draining the sump, you need a much bigger dish."

"I assume your workshop would be locked up at night?"

"Of course. There's a lot of valuable and dangerous equipment in there. Some of the machinery is especially dangerous."

"So, when did you lock the workshop on Monday?"

Jackson thought for a moment. "I went in there in the morning for an hour and locked up at lunchtime. I had no need to go back to the workshop for the rest of the day. In theory we should still be on holiday."

"Could anyone have got in to use your equipment?"

"I shouldn't think so. The only spare set of keys is kept in the school office. All the spare keys are kept there. The School Secretary guards them with her life. She's a bit of a dragon, but I suppose you've met her already."

The Bear ignored the clumsy attempt at humour. This was far too important. "And your own keys," he said, "they could not have been borrowed?"

"Hardly." Jackson stood up and jingled a bunch of keys which was attached to his belt. "It's only when I take my trousers off," he said, "that these leave me. I don't even take the key off the ring when I use it. And, before you ask, I only took my trousers off when I went to bed."

"So, you are probably the only person other than this Jessie person who could have gone to your own workshop, found the tray in question, cut the brake line and returned everything to its place." Jackson stared at him in disbelief. It had not really crossed his mind until that moment that he was a suspect. His relaxed manner changed abruptly.

"You accusing me of murder, or Jessie? Why the hell would I want to kill this Muncaster man? Jessie never even knew him"

"That is a question only you could answer," said The Bear, "but here is a suggestion for you to think over: the new headmaster had suggested your department might be destined for closure. You appeared likely to lose your job, your rent-free flat, which I am given to believe is above the workshop itself, and a very pleasant number, in that you have the use of a well-equipped workshop. You are a member of the teaching staff, and that means you have ten or twelve weeks' holiday a year. Need I go on?"

"Before you are so bloody insulting," Jackson replied, "at least get your facts straight. I am a very well qualified mechanic with a degree and a teaching certificate. I could easily find work either as a teacher somewhere else or as a mechanic. As for its being a cushy number, I do the job because I like teaching kids. The flat is far from rent-free, in fact it's a bit on the expensive side in my opinion, considering that it is only rudimentary. And if you think the job means so much to me that I would actually endanger some poor bugger's life, you are absolutely wrong. When I heard that there was a possibility the workshop would be closed, I made a couple of phone calls. I have a job waiting for me, if I want it. You'd better look elsewhere for your murderer."

"Thank you, Mr Jackson, that will be all for now. I may want to ask you some further questions. Please let us know if you think of anything that could be helpful, such as colleagues who have shown a great interest in using the equipment. If you notice some of the equipment has been moved, let us know."

Jackson gave him a withering glance and strode to the door.

The Bear picked up the phone and spoke to Irma Beauchamp. "Mrs Beauchamp," he said, "can you tell me how much rent Mr Jackson pays for his flat?"

There was a moment's silence. "You mean Cliff Jackson, our car man?"

"Of course, who do you think, Stonewall Jackson?"

"I don't know what he pays," said Irma. "Do you want me to ask my husband?"

"Yes, ask your husband." The Bear was irritated. He heard Irma speak to Frank Beauchamp and the Bursar's puzzled response, "What does he want to know that for? Tell him I'll have to look it up."

"I'll ring you back with the information," said Irma. "He has to look it up."

The Bear was thinking Frank Beauchamp seemed to be an efficient man at his job, and the thought made him wonder how the school had become so financially threatened. Surely, the Bursar must have seen the problems some time ago, so, why had he not flagged them up more successfully until now when it was almost too late? Meanwhile, there were yet more statements to be perused. Someone must visit this Jessie woman to check Jackson's alibi.

Chapter three

In place of the blackboard and easel, the police had set up an official-looking noticeboard in the entrance hall. Gordon checked it to see if he was required for anything, but his name did not appear. He was at a loose end. He had completed mowing all the grass, although no one had told him to continue with the job. Like everybody else, he had to remain within reach, just in case the Chief Inspector decided to call for him. He felt intensely frustrated. It was like being in a prison camp, one without walls or even barbed wire. One or two of the residents were prepared to break out. Stephen Wilder was one of the first. He could not exist without a drink, and he saw no reason not to continue his daily visits to the local pub. Others, like Thelma Black, decided that they needed shopping, principally food shopping, and lost no time, once the wreckage had been removed from the driveway, in heading for the local town.

Gordon had nowhere to go. His early morning run was a welcome escape, but it was over before breakfast. He decided to sort out the contents of the groundsman's hut. The weather was dry, so he could move at least some of the contents outside to make room. He also found the wherewithal to repair or repaint some of the equipment. He knew that this might well be a complete waste of time, if the school was not to reopen at all, but it gave him something to do. The hut had not been given a spring clean for a long time, so the floor had gathered a lot of weeds, dead leaves and other rubbish. With a yard broom Gordon swept all this out. He even cleaned the old Ferguson tractor. It kept him busy for several days. It also meant that he was not compelled to spend much of his time with his new colleagues, most of whom were poor company. Not only were they anxious about the threat of redundancy, even now that the principal stirrer of the long spoon, Mulcaster, had been removed, they were resentful. The intensely critical remarks he had made about the quality of teaching and of the school itself stung and lingered unpleasantly in their minds. Their conversations were dominated by this resentment, and Gordon was happy not to be part of it.

He broached the subject with Beth, as they took their morning exercise. Like him, Beth preferred not to be involved in the depressing conversations.

"What will be, will be," she said. "I have other things on my mind. It's Gran I'm concerned with. She really is not well. There's no way I can persuade her to move from her home."

"Where exactly does she live?" Gordon asked. "You told me it was about a quarter of a mile from the bridge."

"If you've got nothing better to do," Beth said, "why don't you do the extra half mile with me? Gran would be quite pleased to have an unexpected visitor. She doesn't see many."

"Are you sure? I don't want to intrude."

Beth laughed. "Don't worry about that," she said. "It would probably do her good. I'm worried about the fact that she is so isolated."

"Is she on the phone?"

"No. They would have to put in a special line, and she refuses to pay."

"I can understand why you're worried. Isn't there anyone else in the family who could visit her like you?"

"No, not regularly, anyway. My brother tries to get there when he can, but he's busy. He's a journalist, older than me, and doing well, but he has to chase all over the place."

"What's his name"

"John."

They jogged on and crossed the bridge. They turned left, downstream, and were soon running through woodland. It was very pleasant. The morning was cool, but the exercise was keeping them warm. It was mixed woodland, mostly broad-leafed trees, and there were numerous birds. It took only a few minutes to reach the cottage. It faced away from them. The remains of a vegetable garden led to the back door. Beth led the way, opened the door, and called out to her grandmother before going inside. Gordon waited at the door. After a moment, Beth reappeared and told him to come in.

He was in a little passageway with the kitchen on his right. The living room was a matter of two steps further on. He followed Beth inside.

Beth's Gran was sitting in a large chair, a rug over her knees. A large, ginger cat slept on the rug. A few feet in front of her was the open hearth. This was made of stone. The fireplace was wide, and iron basket held the burning logs, but the wood crackled and sparked, throwing red embers on the stones. This was doubly dangerous because four more cats lay close to the fire.

"Don't your cats ever catch fire?" Gordon asked, half joking.

"Oh, yes. They get their fur singed quite a lot. It's the long-haired one that's the nuisance," said Gran. "I've had to put out the flames sometimes."

Beth was watching Gordon, waiting to see how he got on with her Gran. He was amused.

"They love the warmth," she said. "Can I offer you a cup of tea? Beth will have to make it."

"No, thank you very much. We still have to run all the way back to the school," said Gordon.

"How have you been, Gran?" asked Beth.

"I am all right. I don't know why you make such a fuss. I'm not as fit as I once was, I couldn't run like you, not these days, but I can look after myself."

"Well, it's my job to worry about you," said Beth. "You're on your own all day, don't you get lonely?"

"I've got the cats," her Gran replied, "and I listened to the wireless quite a lot. And I see you every morning. I have lived here ever since I married your grandad. I'm used to it."

"What if you get poorly?"

"I'm as fit as a fiddle – well, almost."

"Can we do anything for you?"

"You can pump me some water before you go."

Beth led Gordon back through the door they had come in by. Attached to the wall was a wooden handle, about two feet long. She seized it and moved it from side to side. It was attached to a pipe which ran down into a borehole and fed a storage tank inside the cottage.

"It takes about sixty turns," she said, and then stood aside so that Gordon could take over. It was not especially hard work, although his arm began to ache a little by the time he had finished.

They did not stay long, but the old woman was obviously pleased by the visit. They bade her goodbye and began the run back to the school.

"I can understand why you're worried," Gordon said. "She has no way of calling for help in an emergency. That fireplace worries me."

"That doesn't really worry me any more," said Beth. "I'm much more worried that she should have a fall.

She could be lying on the floor or even in the garden for hours."

"What about the Welfare?"

"I've tried to suggest they could provide carers at least twice a day. She won't have any of it. She even gets angry when I suggest it."

"Surely, one of these days, she'll have to accept that she needs help."

"I dare you try to persuade her!"

"How old is she?"

"Eighty-eight."

Gordon whistled. They crossed the bridge without stopping, and they were soon back at the school. As they reached the top of the field, they passed the old Steward's House, now occupied by Frank and Irma Beauchamp.

There were two or three such houses, which had been built at the same time as the school. There was the Steward's House, the Gardener's House, the Groom's House and the Master's House. Over the years there had been changes. The Steward's House was occupied appropriately by the school Bursar. The Master's House, where the first Headmaster had lived, was superseded by a flat in the main building. The house itself was now occupied by Harold and Thelma Black, Beth explained. It gave Thelma a sense of superiority, boosting her snobbishness. The Gardener's House still housed the gardener, but there was now just one man, so the building had been converted into two flats, one of which had been allocated to Gordon. Once the horses had been replaced by cars, the Carriage house, where the carriages had been stored, was itself converted and the Head of Mechanical Engineering lived there in another flat. The Groom's House was thus available for others to occupy. Currently, it was where Raymond and Jenny Carpenter lived. All this was at first very confusing. The Steward's House, occupied by the Beauchamps, had a large garden, as had the neighbouring Master's House. Both gardens were screened by fences.

"I'll never remember all that," said Gordon.

Beth laughed. "You will get used to it in time," she said, but they were both wondering if they would in fact have much time.

Later that afternoon, Gordon, who had been busy repainting a set of hurdles, straightened his back and took a few steps along the path by the river to stand and stare at the little wood. He was thinking to himself it would be good to have a pair of binoculars. There were lots of birds, not all of which he could identify, and there were others on the water. There were at least three kinds of ducks. He realised he was quite ignorant on the subject.

He was all at once aware that someone was approaching along the path from among the trees. It was one of the teachers. Gordon recognised him by sight. He was a head of department, but which department he did not know. He was a short man, trim, even athletic. He wore a camouflage jacket and he had binoculars around his neck.

"Hello," he said, "I didn't know you were a twitcher."

"A what?" Gordon did not know the word.

"A twitcher, a birdwatcher."

"Oh! Not really, though I'm thinking I could get interested. There seem to be a lot of birds around here."

"Quite a lot," the newcomer agreed. "My name is Williams, by the way. You're the new boy, the tractor driver. Sorry, I don't know your name."

Gordon introduced himself. "Do you teach science?" he asked, thinking it a reasonable deduction.

Williams laughed, "No," he said, "I'm in charge of English. Ornithology is just a hobby."

They stood in companionable silence, looking at the scene before them.

"If you are really interested," Williams said, "if you get away from the school a little, downstream is probably best. There's more to see in the woods, not only birds, but some of the other wildlife. There's even a badge's sett in there. Mind you, if you want to see the badgers, you need to be about at dusk or very early in the morning."

"Maybe I should do my early morning run that way," said Gordon. "So far, I have only run upstream."

"Aha! You're one of those, are you? A long-distance runner?"

"Not exactly," Gordon replied. "I like to keep in shape, so I always go for a run in the morning. I've discovered someone else does the same."

"You must mean the admirable Miss Shepherd."

"Of course, you will know her."

"Yes, she seems a very nice young woman. We don't have much to do with one another in the normal course of events, but we do both have a habit of getting out and about early in the morning. Now, it seems, there will be three of us. Speak of the devil!"

Beth had just walked down the sports field from the school, seemingly heading for the river. She greeted both men.

"I was just saying," Williams told her, "that we three all seem to be early risers. Mr – sorry, I don't remember your name –"

"Drake," Gordon prompted him.

"Mr Drake – I ought to remember that, oughtn't I?"

Beth smiled. "Gordon and I have already agreed to go running together. Why don't you join us?"

"Run?" Williams looked disconcerted. "I never run these days. I do a fair bit of walking, but I'm a little too old to take up running. Thanks for the invitation."

With that, he bade them farewell and strode off towards the school.

"Seems like a nice chap," Gordon observed.

"Yes, he is. He's an interesting man, too. I've been told he had a challenging time during the war. He was awarded the Military Cross, I was told, though I don't know what for. He always seems very quiet but he's a first-class teacher. The boys love him."

"Married?"

"No."

"What brings you down here, anyway?"

"I'm restless," said Beth, turning, as if to prove her words, to look across the river towards the woods on the other side. "I can't help worrying about Gran."

"She seemed very bright to me."

"Mentally, perhaps, but you must admit she is quite frail and vulnerable."

"Surely, living as she does is her choice."

"Yes, you're right, but I think I've seen a deterioration in the last couple of weeks especially. I can't help worrying about her."

"You can't do much more. You visitor every day."

"Anything could happen in twenty-four hours," Beth replied. She continued to stare in the direction of her grandmother's cottage on the other side of the trees. "I have a strange sort of premonition. It's probably nonsense, but I think I'll pay her another visit this evening. I'd never be able to sleep otherwise."

"When you say this evening," Gordon said, "it will be dark by about seven o'clock."

"I'm not afraid of the dark."

"It sounds a bit dodgy. You don't know who you could meet. Don't forget somebody here managed to bring about the new headmaster's death. Whoever he is, he is still at large."

"Whoever he is," Beth repeated," he can't have any argument with me."

"Would you object if I came with you? I'd feel a little happier."

Beth turned and looked at him. "OK, if you insist, but you really don't need to."

"What time?"

"About eight o'clock. She goes to bed quite early. That's another thing: she relies on paraffin lamps, no electricity. I know she's used them all her life, but I also think they are an accident waiting to happen."

"Right, I'll meet you down here with a torch."

He left Beth, still gazing across the water, and he returned to his painting.

He made his way down to the river at the time they had agreed. It was a cloudy night and a crescent moon flitted in and out, leaving a faint gleam to indicate the water. The path was barely detectable in places. He could see well enough to keep to the path until the moon was hidden. He was glad he had brought a torch.

Beth joined him within a minute, padding silently over the grass.

"Let's go," was all she said, and led the way. She moved more quickly than in the morning.

"Steady!" Gordon warned. "Don't trip."

"If you can't keep up," she said over her shoulder, "go back. I'll be OK. It's Gran I'm worried about."

After that he said nothing but concentrated on keeping pace with her. They reached the bridge quickly and were soon entering the trees. Now it was truly dark and even Beth was glad of the light of the torch. Without it, Gordon would not have seen the garden gate. There was no light from the cottage, but Beth had explained there was no electricity. No doubt the paraffin lamps could only be seen from the other side. Beth said nothing as they reached the back door. Gordon shone his torch on the latch and Beth went in, calling out as she went. Gordon followed.

The only light came from the fireplace. There were two logs glowing red. Several startled cats scuttled out of the way as Beth uttered an inarticulate cry. The old woman lay on the floor, mercifully clear of the fire, but near enough to be warm

"There's a lamp on the table," said Beth, as she knelt beside her grandmother.

Gordon found the lamp and a box of matches. He succeeded in lighting the wick. It gave off more light than he expected, and he moved it nearer the edge of the table.

"Is she..?"

"I think she may have had a stroke," said Beth. "We have to get her help."

"There's no phone!"

"If I stay with her, can you run back to the school and phone for an ambulance? It's the nearest phone. Be as quick as you can, please."

"The address?"

"What? Oh, of course!" Beth left her grandmother for a moment and took an envelope from a small pile on the table. She took out the contents and handed Gordon the envelope. "Go!" she said.

He took the torch and made his way out of the garden, back onto the path. He ran as fast as he dared, but it felt like a long journey. As his feet drummed on the wooden bridge, he feared the worst, and he was relieved to reach the playing field. The lights were still on inside the school as he ran down the corridor to the entrance hall. A policeman was pinning a new notice on the board.

"What's the hurry?" he asked.

"An old lady," Gordon gasped. "A stroke."

"What old lady?"

Gordon held out the envelope. It was the policeman's turn to run. Gordon followed him to Classroom Number one. Within seconds he had alerted an ambulance to go to the Gamekeeper's Cottage in Five Acre Wood. Then he handed the envelope back to Gordon.

"Well done, lad," he said. "Sit down and have a cup of tea."

Gordon was glad to do so. "Where will they take her?" he asked, as his breathing slowed.

"Most likely to Horsham. It'll take quite a while to get to her if I know anything. Is there someone with her?"

Gordon explained as clearly as he could.

"If I were you, I'd give it an hour, then ring the hospital. Not much you can do, mind. I take it this Miss Shepherd will go with her grandma to the hospital?"

"I imagine she will."

At 10.15 Gordon spoke to someone at the hospital. He explained who he was, and he asked how Mrs Peacock was."

"Are you a relative?"

"No."

"Then, I'm afraid I can't give you any information."

"Oh!" He had not expected that. "Mrs Peacock's granddaughter came in the ambulance with her. Can I speak to Miss Shepherd?"

The operator must have put her hand over the mouthpiece. Gordon heard a muffled conversation, but no distinguishable words. At last, "This is highly irregular, so please keep it short."

"Gordon?"

"Beth? How is she?"

"Not good. We don't know how long she was lying there. Thank you for your help." She was very distressed. Her voice was unsteady.

"Have you alerted the rest of the family?"

"There isn't anyone except John, and I don't know where he is exactly. My parents are abroad."

"That's terrible. Hold on, I'll drive over."

"There's no need to do that. You've been kind enough already."

"You're going to need a lift home if nothing else. Give me an hour."

Beth made a weak attempt to put him off, but she was in no fit state to think clearly. Gordon put the phone down and went back to his flat. There he made a flask of tea, cheese sandwiches and two chocolate bars. Since it was a chilly night, he took an old, clean, travelling rug and a huge, old sweater, and took everything to his little car. It started without trouble, and he drove warily down to the main road. He reached the hospital shortly before midnight, explained himself to the surprised night porter and so to the ward where he found Beth sitting on a bench in the corridor. She was in tears.

"Thank you for coming," she said." I…"

She got no further, and Gordon sat next to her and put a comforting arm round her shoulders as she gave way to a fit of weeping. She wiped her eyes and tried to apologise.

Gordon stopped her. "How is she?" he asked.

"She didn't make it," Beth said. "She never regained consciousness. The nurses are in there now, tidying up."

"I'm so sorry," said Gordon. "What are you going to do?"

"I'm waiting until they've finished, then I want to sit with her for a while. There's no need for you to wait."

"I'll wait until you're ready, then I'll drive you home. It's not as though I've got other things to do. You won't want to talk, but you may find it helps to have company."

"Thank you."

Two nurses emerged from the ward. One held the door open and told Beth she could go and sit by the bed to make her goodbyes. She stood, stiff-backed and dignified, and walked swiftly in. The two nurses nodded to Gordon and walked off as far as an area behind a high counter. Gordon settled for a long wait.

In fact, he only waited about thirty minutes. They walked through the silent corridors and emerged into the darkness of the car park. Gordon did not want to intrude on Beth's grief, so did not speak. He drove out of the hospital and back to Greenacres. The road was quiet, just an occasional vehicle flashed past. He drove up the winding driveway to the back of the school.

"I don't want to go in yet," Beth said, surprising him. "Can we sit in the car for a while?"

"Of course." He manoeuvred the car so that it looked down towards the river. The clouds had blown over. It was cold, but there was no sound. There was a little light from the moon and stars and, to their right, hidden from the rest of the buildings, an outside light picked out the Beauchamps' back yard.

Beth shivered. Gordon reached back and found the rug and the shopping bag containing the flask. He poured a cup of tea, which she accepted gratefully.

"Hungry?" he asked.

"Now you ask," she replied, "I am. It seems wrong."

Gordon gave her a sandwich.

"What time is it?" she asked.

He peered at his watch. It was 2.40.

"What are the Beauchamps doing at this hour?" Beth asked.

"No idea," said Gordon. "You can't see much behind that fence."

The activity went on for a long time. At last the light went out. Gordon checked his watch. It was 3.30 am. By now Beth was asleep, her head against the car window. Gordon was beginning to feel cramp. Cautiously, he opened the door and stepped out into the cold night. It was too cold to stand still, so he stepped onto the grass and walked as far as the Steward's House. He peered through a crack in the fence. The Beauchamps' campervan was no more than a yard away. He was looking directly into a side window. On top of the cupboards that lined the walls he could see cardboard boxes had been placed. One of them had split. It contained books or files of some sort. He realised all at once that he was spying, and he turned away guiltily and went back to the car. Beth had not moved, but she woke as he slipped into his own seat beside her.

"What time is it?" she asked.

"Coming up to four o'clock."

"I'm so sorry," she said. "I've kept you up all night. I should get back to my flat."

"Are you all right?"

She smiled, "Yes, much better," she said. "But thank you for keeping me company. I think we might skip the run this morning, but I'll need to see to the cats. I'm going to be very busy, I imagine."

"I'll feed the cats," said Gordon.

"Oh, would you? I need to get back to the hospital and – what do they say? – make the arrangements for the funeral."

"If you need a hand or a lift, just ask. I'm not going anywhere."

"Thank you," she said, opening the door. "I'll be in touch." With that, she leaned over and kissed him on the cheek, then she was gone, moving silently into the shadows.

To avoid disturbing anyone, Gordon left the car where it was and walked back to his flat and went to bed. He did not expect to sleep, but he did. When he woke it was eleven o'clock. He made himself a cup of coffee then set off at a leisurely pace to feed the cats.

He found a supply of cat food, washed-up the dirty dishes and put out more food. Then, with nothing else to do, he tidied up the sitting room and the bedroom. He cleaned out the fireplace but didn't know what to do with the ashes. In the end he found an old bucket in which he carried them down the garden. He looked at the neglected garden which had once provided quantities of fresh vegetables. Old Mrs Peacock had no longer been able to look after the beds. It all looked quite sad, and Gordon found himself thinking morbid thoughts about the fragility of human life – very unusual for him. He finished the jobs he had set himself and returned to Greenacres. This time he ran hard. The exercise did him a great deal of good, cheering him up. He wondered what Beth would do about the cottage. He assumed her grandmother had owned it. Would Beth inherit it? It was miles from anywhere. He wondered who would want to buy it.

Back at the school, he checked the new, police noticeboard. There was nothing on it which related to him. Then it occurred to him to check the pigeonholes in which post which had been delivered was placed. He had not thought to look in them before. Under the letter D he found a fat envelope addressed to him. It was typewritten. He opened it. It came from a firm of solicitors who announced they were working on behalf of Miss Sandra Embury. Gordon put the letter back inside the envelope and walked out to his car to read it in privacy. The car was still parked where he had left it the previous night. As he took his seat behind the wheel and looked at the pleasant scene across the playing field and the river beyond, he recalled the unusual vigil he had spent with Beth. He wondered how she was getting on. He liked her. She was very capable and normally appeared to be very much in control. Last night had, however, been exceptional, and he had seen her when she was vulnerable.

He took the letter out of the envelope and read it. It was much as he had expected, except that the solicitor had quoted a figure for the proposed maintenance of Sandra and her child. Gordon gasped: it represented nearly one third of his salary. Up to this point his guilt had prepared him to accept whatever conditions were suggested. Now self-preservation took over. He could not afford to pay this much. He would have to contest it. Until he received this letter, he had not thought he would engage in any kind of battle, let alone a legal battle, with Sandra. Guilt was replaced by a certain amount of indignation. If not Sandra herself, then the solicitor working on her behalf had opened a kind of war. Gordon was happy to be reasonable on his terms, but he was not prepared to be reduced to poverty. He would fight. If he managed somehow to find a better paid post in the future, he might be prepared to offer more, but for the present he would reject this claim.

He was surprised by his own reaction. It was a long time since he had felt confident enough to challenge Sandra. Until now he had been overwhelmed by his own responsibility, but he reminded himself, it takes two to make a baby. Sandra had assured him that she was "on the pill" and, since he also used a condom, he thought they were quite safe. And it was not as though Sandra had not participated with enthusiasm. She had to take some responsibility, he told himself.

He put the letter back in the envelope, started the engine, and parked the car in his usual place. As he reversed, the fence at the back of the Steward's House was in full view. He remembered how the Beauchamps had spent some time loading their campervan in the night with cardboard boxes. Why would they choose to dispose of papers and files in the middle of the night? It was quite strange.

Time hung heavily on his hands. He was not inclined to spend too much time mixing with his colleagues, most of whom seemed disgruntled and negative. There were exceptions. Raymond Carpenter was generally affable, as was Williams, but several of the more senior members of staff seemed to have disappeared.

Another notice appeared on the school noticeboard.

> "We have been told that the police investigation is likely to continue for at least three weeks. It will not be practicable to have the boys back while this is going on. That means that term cannot restart before October 3. The office staff and the senior staff are all busy informing parents. We shall keep everybody informed of the consequences, whatever they are."

Gordon frowned, not sure what the last sentence implied. In view of what the Chairman of

Governors and the ill-fated Mulcaster had said, could this be the end of the school? He had a contract by the terms of which he was entitled to two months' notice, but he might be out of work before Christmas! He would also have to leave his flat. He had not as yet had time to grow attached to it, but he did not want to return to live with his mother and stepfather. John was all right in small doses, but Gordon knew the relationship would soon become fragile, if they shared the same roof, especially of he was out of work.

Other members of staff must be similarly worried, some more so, especially if they had lived in Greenacres for several years. He knew very little about them, except for Beth. Her parents were abroad, she said. Was there a family home somewhere? But she was also confident she could easily find another job.

He was beginning to think about her too often.

"Mr Drake!" Gordon turned to see Irma Beauchamp at the door to the office. "Can we have a word, please?"

Gordon followed her inside. He realised there was nowhere for a visitor to sit, making visits uncomfortable. The Bursar was in his usual place.

"Mr Drake," Irma resumed, "I'm sure you were told where the staff car park is."

"Yes, you showed me the day I arrived."

"We noticed you parked your car at the edge of the grass."

"Ah, yes. I returned late from Horsham with Miss Shepherd. Her grandmother was taken into hospital. She died, and Miss Shepherd was upset. She wanted to sit outside for a while. It was very late, so I left the car where it was until later in the day. It wasn't in anyone's way."

"I see. We'll say no more about it in the circumstances, but in future, please use the space allocated."

It seemed strange. Why such a fuss about so little? Gordon began wondering if there was some connection with the goings-on in the Beauchamps' back yard.

The uncertainties and disturbances of the past three days were having an effect. That evening he was unable to sleep. He dressed warmly and let himself out and took a walk round the field. It was dark again, with just enough light to see his way down to the river. He could hear the slight bubbling and lapping sounds but the water itself was invisible. He wondered if fish slept at night. He did not stay long; it was getting chilly, so he walked back across the field and was fifty yards or so from the back of the Steward's House, when the outside light came on again. It would be embarrassing to be seen, so he hung back. He heard the whine of a starter motor and then the quiet purring of a diesel motor. The outside light was turned off. Headlights were switched on and the campervan pulled out. The lights were dipped. The van turned away from the service road and drove over the grass behind the three houses, heading towards the far side of the main building, only the small pool of light from the dipped headlamps betraying its whereabouts. Gordon was far enough away to remain unseen. He was curious to know why the van driver chose to drive over grass. It could only be to avoid being seen, surely. At the far end of the school building the van stopped, and Gordon could just make out the shapes of three women in long dresses, leading small children by the hand. They climbed into the back of the van and drove off, heading across the grass and presumably aiming for the main road at the end of the drive.

What on earth was that all about, he wondered, and who were the women and children?

Chapter four

The Bear was unhappy. The enquiry was unearthing information about some of the residents, but nothing conclusive. He wanted hard evidence, preferably eye-witness reports, which would identify the person who had cut the brake pipes on Mulcaster's car. The vehicle had been parked at night in such a place that whoever had dealt with it could easily have escaped detection by a casual passer-by. So far, no one had stated they had been anywhere near. There was no forensic evidence to help him. Virtually everyone who lived on the Greenacres site had access. Mulcaster was the only driver of a Rover 2000. It was unthinkable that this was a case of mistaken identity.

The investigation must, therefore, proceed by means of the most unsatisfactory hunt for an individual or for individuals with a credible motive. Until all the statements had been collected and analysed, and the most suspicious people interviewed, The Bear had to keep an open mind, but he had already begun to draw up a mental list and to underline some names. One which stood out at present was Stephen Wilder. The jobs of other Heads of Department were doubtless under threat, including the mechanic, Clifford Jackson, but surely Wilder's antipathy was based on a far stronger and older experience. He made no attempt to disguise his hatred for the man he believed responsible for the deaths of eleven men in his, Wilder's platoon. But was Wilder playing a game of double bluff, presenting himself as the principal suspect? Jackson might be in danger of losing his job, as well as his accommodation, but that seemed an insufficient threat to justify homicide. He, above all, would know just how lethal the severing of the brake pipes could be, and Jackson was familiar with the workshops, with access to tools, including a tray in which to collect the tell-tale oil. Other heads of department were threatened in general terms, but only one other department was almost certain to face closure, and that was Domestic Science. Young Beth Shepherd would probably lose her position, if Mulcaster had his way, but The Bear could not believe she would stoop to manslaughter.

The Bear shifted uneasily in the Headmaster's chair. He needed physical evidence, but it looked as though he would have to continue with speculations based on theory and hope the hard evidence would follow. It could take a long time. He was fully aware that he and his men (and women, he reminded himself) were regarded more as interlopers than as helpers. Interviews and statements were stiff with resentment. He was not unduly concerned by this – it was a quite normal part of the job – but it sometimes made it harder to grind out the truth. Irma Beauchamp and her husband, with whom he was in daily contact, seemed to embody this resentment. They both provided him with factual information, when asked, but they seemed slow at times. It was as though they were telling him that the business of Greenacres School was not for him to penetrate.

He picked up the phone and spoke to Sir Lionel.

"Can you tell me when the school last a general inspection had?" he asked.

Sir Lionel sounded surprised. "A full-blown inspection? I really don't remember. Several years."

"Where can I find the report?"

"Really, Chief Inspector, what on earth could that have to do with your enquiry?"

"I don't know, but I'd like sight of it."

Sir Lionel was a long time thinking. "Now I come to think about it," he said, "I don't think it ever came off."

"Never came off? What does that mean?"

"The procedure for private schools is rather different," Sir Lionel explained. "Her Majesty's Inspectorate waits to be invited to visit. I remember now, we – the Governors, that is – discussed issuing such an invitation, but the new Bursar was just taking over. He pointed out that it might be better to wait until the reorganisation was complete."

"You mean you have never had an official inspection?"

There was an embarrassed silence before Sir Lionel admitted in a quiet voice, "Well, no, I suppose we haven't."

The Bear put down the phone, looking shocked. He sat for a while in thought, then called his Superintendent.

"Progress, Ted?"

He was not sure there was any. "Not really, sir," he reported, and explained the problems. "There is one suspect so far, but no hard evidence. We're still trying to establish motives. Almost everyone on site had the opportunity. No eye-witnesses. This is going to be difficult. But that's not why I called."

"Oh?"

"The more we look into this school, the stranger things we find. I want to find out why the groundsman handed in his notice suddenly at the end of term, for a start. I'm also curious about the Punjabis being employed, especially since they seem to have their dependents with them. Are they legitimate? But there has been no official inspection of the school for as long as I can find out."

"Do you think the quality of the teaching has anything to do with the murder? That seems highly improbable."

"I suppose it does, but there's definitely something wrong."

"It sounds as if your nose is twitching, trying to sniff out a trail."

"You're probably right, sir."

"Nothing substantive, then?"

"No, just a lot of loose ends so far."

"Suspects?"

"Two possibly; there's Stephen Wilder, Head of Maths. He's an alcoholic who would have lost the job a long time ago if his godfather wasn't Chairman of the Governors."

"That sounds highly irregular. What's the connection with Mulcaster?"

"I hope we can check it out. It seems Mulcaster was the intelligence officer whose misinformation led Wilder and his platoon into an ambush. Wilder was the only survivor. The result was a nervous breakdown for Wilder."

"That certainly sounds like a motive. You sound unsure, though."

"Partly because Wilder told me most of this himself. You'd have thought he would try to hide it, unless it's a double bluff. But the man is in such a state, I'm not convinced he could think up such a plan."

"What plan, the murder, you mean?"

"No, the bluff."

"Who is the second suspect?"

"The man in charge of the workshop. He is a trained mechanic and he had been told by Mulcaster he was likely to be out of a job. He would also lose his flat. He has the skill necessary to cut the brake line and get rid of the fluid. He says he could easily find another job. I don't like the man, though."

"Your Wilder sounds a better candidate."

"Yes, other teachers' jobs were also under threat, but I can't really see that as reason to want to injure or kill Mulcaster."

"It sounds as though you need to do a lot more digging yet."

"I'm afraid so. That adds another complication."

"What's that?"
"The Governors and the Acting Headmaster and maybe the School Bursar, tell me the very survival of the school is under threat. Apparently, they have financial problems, though they have never even had a school inspection. It's not just the quality of the teaching."

"I see. Any idea what kind of difficulties?"

"They suggest that falling numbers mean the income is inadequate."

"They can't just put up their fees?"

"I don't really understand these things, sir. Maybe we need a specialist to look into it."

The Super did not answer immediately. Then he commented, "You don't think this is something for the Fraud Squad?"

It was The Bear's turn to hesitate. "I really don't know, sir. Of course, Mulcaster would have sorted that out if he had had the time. He was a qualified accountant."

"Ah! You think there could be a connection?"

"I just don't know. This is not a straightforward case, that much is obvious. Hard, physical evidence doesn't exist, and that leaves us groping around, searching for motives first. Just about anybody at the school could have done it."

"Do your best, Ted. You'll get there in the end. I'll make a few calls to see if we can't find someone with financial expertise. You might get this Bursar fellow..."

"Beauchamp."

"Yes, Beauchamp to get the books ready for an inspection to save time."

"Thank you, sir."

The Bear put down the phone and swivelled in the comfortable chair to look out of the window. Across the narrow road at the side of the building the short, grassy verge was surmounted by a laurel bush. It was restful on the eyes, but The Bear was not conscious of it, nor of the small birds that flitted past. He was frowning, hating the feeling of bafflement. He stood up and left the office in search of Sergeant Rawlings.

He found him listening to one of the constables.

"OK," he said, "no need to make a fuss about it, just ask the people who live round the back. It's probably something and nothing, but well done for spotting it."

As the young man picked up his helmet and headed for the door, Rawlings turned to The Bear, "Someone drove out of the gates last night or this morning."

"Nothing wrong with that," said The Bear, "this isn't a prison."

"But whoever it was," Rawlings explained, "he drove the long way round over the grass. It's a bit peculiar."

"It's probably nothing, but I'm beginning to think everything about this place is a bit weird."

"You'll sort it out, Boss. You always do."

"Thanks. I wish I felt as confident."

"I've noticed something you probably know about already…"

"What's that?"

"Well, you know you asked for the personal files of all the staff?"

"Yes, Mrs Beauchamp wasn't too pleased. She gave them all to you and insisted on an official receipt."

"Yes, all done. When I finished listing them all, I realised there were two missing."

"What? Whose?" The Bear was alarmed.

"The Beauchamps themselves. I was going to ask you if you already had them."

"No, I haven't got them. That woman! She pretends to be the perfect secretary, ready to work hard to produce the goods, but she wants to be in control. She can't hide information because it relates to her and her husband. They are suspects like everyone else."

"Do you want me to deal with it, Boss?"

"No, leave it with me. I could do with something enjoyable for a change."

"Enjoyable?" But Rawlings knew what was meant.

The Bear helped himself to a mug of tea and a small stack of biscuits before settling down to review the case with Rawlings. Rawlings listened as his boss repeated most of what he had told the Super, for the most part merely nodding to confirm the facts.

"Wilder is the prime suspect," Rawlings remarked. "There can't be much doubt of that."

"It still doesn't sound quite right, though," The Bear replied. "The whole situation is complicated. This place is like a madhouse. There's too much going on. Why did the groundsman leave so suddenly? Was there even anything suspicious about the death of the previous Headmaster? "

"I'll get Pearl Burton to look through the minutes of the Governors' meetings," said

Rawlings. "She's good at boring jobs like that. She may pick up any irregularities."

"Good idea."

"I've already got Rackham looking for the groundsman. We may get to the bottom of his leaving."

"Good. We also need to look much more closely into Stephen Wilder, including the periods he spent drying out."

"They won't tell us much," said Rawlings. "That is classified medical information."

"Maybe, but I'm sure we can find out a lot more. And I am extremely curious about how he was able to track down and identify Mulcaster as the officer responsible for the shambles in which his comrades died."

"That won't be easy, either."

"No."

Chapter five

Gordon heated a kettle on the fire he kindled in the sitting room of the cottage. Two of the cats rubbed against his legs. He felt sorry for them. He wondered how or if they missed the old woman. When the kettle was warm enough, he took it into the kitchen. He had collected the various bowls and thrown out the remaining scraps of food. Now he washed up, found a tea-towel to dry the bowls, and refilled them with cat food from the cupboard. He put down a larger bowl of cold water and stood, hands on hips, watching with an indulgent smile. He wondered whether Beth had thought about the cats. She must have a lot on her mind, dealing with the funeral director. It had not occurred to him until too late that he did not know how to contact her. He did not know where her flat was in the big building. Not that she would welcome him if he went blundering in. Beth was an undemanding companion, quite unlike the girls he had known at uni. Beth was unpretentious, a friend who happened to be female.

He was in no hurry to run back to the school, although he was late this morning. His watch said 9.10 am. Two of the cats, having sniffed at the food, had returned to the sitting room and were curled up on the old sofa, tails over their faces, asleep. Out of curiosity, Gordon went to the front door and opened it with a struggle. It was obviously not used much. The wood was swollen, and stuck, and small plants and grass grew at the bottom. Pushing the door open uprooted them. He stepped out onto the step. This had once been a charming cottage garden. It had been neglected for years, but it was now crowded with every kind of growth. Rose bushes spread, in need of severe pruning. Granny Bonnets, lupins, lilies had once thrived but now battled for survival with unrecognisable plants and dead seed-heads, most of which Gordon thought, were weeds. A dilapidated, picket fence sagged, held upright by the vegetation. A gate in the fence, which had obviously not been used for years, had once led to a rutted track which ran about a hundred yards as far as a field, then it turned right and disappeared behind the outlying trees of the little wood.

He was about to go back inside when he heard an engine. It did not sound like a tractor, but what else could it be? It emerged from the trees, lurching and bumping over the uneven track. It was a green Land Rover and it headed for the

Gamekeeper's Cottage. Gordon remained where he was. The vehicle came to a stop on the other side of the gate. The driver and a passenger got out, two women. They wore green uniforms, rather like those worn by Land Army women during the war.

"Hello!" the driver shouted. "Mr Shepherd?"

"No," Gordon corrected her, "My name's Drake."

"Oh, We've come to collect the cats."

The two women opened the back of the Landrover and brought out wire carrying baskets, then made their way with difficulty through the overgrown garden.

"I've just fed the cats," said Gordon. Miss Shepherd is a friend. It was her grandmother that lived here. I said I'd see they were fed every day."

"Ah!" said the driver. "Did she not tell you she'd asked us to collect the cats?"

"No."

"Well, she did, and we've come to collect them."

"What will happen to them?"

"Our vet will check them out and make sure they're healthy, then we shall do our best to re-home them."

"I see."

"Don't worry, we shall look after them. Are you a cat-lover?"

"No, not really."

"In that case it's good of you to look after them. Can we go in?"

Gordon watched the vehicle make its bumpy way down the track a few minutes later with a strange feeling of loss. What would happen now? This little cottage had been a home, but it was now derelict. The old lady had gone, taking with her memories of friends, family, events. She had doubtless once tended the now overgrown garden with care and love. The garden was now just a tangle, uncared for. The house was dark, cold and without even the cats to give it life. Shutting the door was like closing the cover of a much-loved history book. He would no longer have a reason to come back. All that remained was the brief memory of the old lady in front of the open fire, surrounded by her cats.

He ran back through the wood in a curious mood.

A little later he checked the notices in the entrance hall. There was nothing new. He looked in the pigeon-holes and found a handwritten envelope. There was no stamp on it, so it was presumably someone on the site. He tore the envelope open and saw the signature, Beth. It cheered him, and he sat on the stairs to read the note.

"Dear Gordon,

First, thank you for looking after the cats in the Gamekeeper's Cottage. I have asked the Cats' Welfare people to collect them. They love cats, and they will look after them until they can find homes for them. They said they'd collect them today some time, so you won't need to visit after today. Thank you. Gran would be very grateful.

"I realized you don't know where my flat is. I don't think it would be a good idea for me to visit you in your place; there are a lot of malicious gossips here who would make two and two add up to at least five. I am busy, as you can imagine, but I need to resume my daily run. Perhaps we can go on where we left off. What about joining forces tomorrow? Maybe we could try another route.

I shall go, anyway, at 6.30. See you then, maybe.

Yours,

Beth"

He was pleased to resume the morning run with Beth. Running on his own was all right, but there was an element of competition or at least of rivalry with Beth. He liked the girl. He saw her as a friend, not as a potential girlfriend.

He was ready the following morning a few minutes early, and was doing a few warm-up exercises when Beth joined him on the path. They said hello and Gordon suggested following the river downstream. Beth agreed readily, and they set off at a gentle jog. Neither wanted to start a conversation. The path took them past the groundsman's shed. It looked tidier even on the outside as a result of Gordon's efforts, the doors freed from the grass and weeds which had jammed them. Soon they were in unfamiliar territory. They came to a gate which seemed to mark the boundary of

Greenacres. Beyond the gate the path continued next to the water, but on their left they were skirting a water meadow. Another gate cut the path off from woodland, but they continued. Gordon realized the woodland on this side of the river mirrored that on the other side, beyond which lay the old cottage. Everywhere, there were birds, their songs and the sounds of the stream being the only accompaniment to the padding of their feet. Not far away, a cock pheasant called out in alarm, the sound very loud. Beth was leading at this point, but she suddenly stopped and left the path, walking into the trees.

"Where are you going?" Gordon asked.

"I seem to remember there's a badger sett somewhere here."

They soon found it, the earth had been worn bare, like an old carpet in a small, flat space at the foot of a bank. A large entrance hole gaped.

"Wrong time of day to see any badgers," Beth said. "I'm glad they're still here."

They stood for a while to catch their breath.

"How are things going?" Gordon asked.

"Gran, you mean? I'm still pretty upset. Why do people have to die? That's a silly question. It will probably take me a long time to get used to it. She was so independent – well, bloody-minded is a better word. She did her best never to see a doctor. That has complicated things for everyone, especially me."

Gordon looked at her, awaiting clarification.

"Apparently," Beth explained, "because she hadn't seen a doctor in the past three weeks, the authorities – the coroner, that is – must by law carry out a post-mortem. We can't arrange her funeral until that's done."

"Have you got anyone helping you? Any family members?"

"Not really. My parents are abroad. The only other family member who might help is my brother, John, but he's up to his ears in the latest bit of research."

"Research? He's an academic?"

Beth laughed, "No. He's a journalist. He's five years older than me. He calls himself an investigative journalist."

"Surely, he could spare time to help you."

"It's OK, I can cope. Besides, it keeps me busy, and I was always closer to Gran. He'll help when I really need him, and he'll come to the funeral."

"Would you mind if I came?"

"No, of course not, if you really want to, but you hardly knew her."

"I liked her and I'd like to pay my respects."

"Fine. There won't be many people there. She lived alone for a good few years."

They returned to the path and ran about half a mile further, emerging from the trees into another field in which a herd of black and white cows were returning from a farmyard at the other side.

"Early morning milking," Beth explained. A large farmhouse faced the field, and a man was shutting the gate behind the cattle. He must have seen the two runners but made no sign. They turned back.

"Why are we being so lazy?" asked Beth. "Come on! Race you through the wood."

"Same time tomorrow" Gordon asked, as they reached Greenacres.

"Yes," she replied, "and thank you."

Gordon was genuinely puzzled. "For feeding the cats?"

"No, for keeping me company. I'm feeling rather lost at the moment. Now that Gran's gone, there's nothing much to keep me here. Whatever happens to the school, I won't want to hang around for long, but none of us can make plans at the moment."

"You mean I'll have to go running on my own?"

"Do you think any of us will have a job here once the police investigation is over?"

It was a new thought for Gordon. "Why not?" he asked, thinking what a financial mess would face him. Without a steady income, however small, he would not be able to pay the maintenance to Sandra. He let himself into his flat, his cheerful mood replaced by anxiety.

The police continued to carry out interviews, but no one knew what they were doing. The senior staff members were also rarely to be seen. Gordon understood they were phoning all the parents, trying to keep them up to date, and apologising for the disruption to their sons' education. He overheard worried, frustrated, sometimes angry snatches of conversation which suggested the parents' reaction was frequently angry. In the afternoon of the third day after the crash, Gordon bumped into Raymond Carpenter. He was taking a breather on the grass behind the school, standing with a mug of tea in his hand, and staring into the distance. He acknowledged Gordon's greeting with a nod.

"I've had some enjoyable times here," he said.

"Had? Why the past tense? I know your leg is painful."

"It's not that," said Carpenter. "I'm all but certain the school is finished for good. I doubt we'll reopen at all."

Gordon looked at him anxiously. "Surely," he said, "you can't just shut up shop? There must be laws about it."

Carpenter turned and faced him. He raised his powerful arms in a huge shrug of defeat and despair. "I've spoken to eleven parents so far," he said, "and the others say the same. Mulcaster's death and the police investigation have made them all hostile. They don't say so in as many words, but they blame us, the staff. It's obvious that the accident was no such thing, so we are all tarred with the same brush."

"Don't you think it will blow over, once they find who's responsible?"

Carpenter threw the remaining contents of his mug on the grass. "No," he said. "There won't be enough pupils left to keep the place afloat financially. I'm afraid you'd better start looking for another job."

With that, he turned and limped back to the school. Gordon stared after him, feeling very uneasy.

A uniformed policeman crossed the grass and approached him. "Are you Mr Drake?" he asked.

"Yes," What now, Gordon wondered.

"Sorry to bother you, sir," said the policeman. He was young, no older than Gordon. "I believe you have a flat in the Gardener's House?"

"Yes," said Gordon. "Don't tell me there's been a break-m!"

"No, nothing like that. We're asking the people who live in the various houses the same question, but I seem to have missed you on three occasions."

"What question?"

"You have a car here?"

"Yes, a bit of an old banger, but it's OK."

"Did you take it out on Monday night!"

"Yes, I did. I drove into Horsham to collect Miss Shepherd from hospital."

"Oh, I'm sorry. I didn't know she was ill."

"She wasn't." Gordon explained.

"I see," said the young man, who was writing in his notebook. " And did you by any chance drive across the frass?"

"When we got back from the hospital," Gordon explained, "I drove onto the field here and we sat and talked for a while."

"On this part of the field?"

"Yes, why?"

"Did you drive over the grass on the other side of the main building?"

"No." Gordon frowned as he thought about that night. "Come to think about it," he said, "I did see someone drive round that way in the middle of the night."

"But you didn't report it?"

"None of my business," said Gordon. "He wasn't breaking the law, driving at night."

"You said 'he'," observed the constable. "Do you know who this was?"

"Yes, it was Mr Beauchamp, the Bursar."

"Would you mind coming back into the Operations Room with me, sir? I'm sure Sergeant Rawlings would like to hear about this. We can take a statement there."

"OK, though I don't see how this will help your enquiries."

But Sergeant Rawlings was indeed interested. He was also interested to hear how Beauchamp had picked up the women and children and taken them away.

"There's something else," Gordon said, when Rawlings was thanking him for his statement.

"Something else?"

"It may be something or nothing, but it's certainly odd."

"But you didn't think to tell us?"

"No. Well, I was sort of ashamed."

"Ashamed? About what?"

Gordon described how he had seen both the Beauchamps loading boxes of papers into their campervan."

"Ashamed or not," Rawlings observed, "you should have told us about this before."

Gordon felt extremely ill at ease. He had not been reprimanded by Rawlings for spying on a colleague. He did not want to be drawn into other people's secrets. He could not hazard the least guess to link all this with the death of Mulcaster. He may have caused the police to investigate the two most hard-pressed members of staff, when, according to Raymond Carpenter, everyone's future was under threat. Rawlings was obviously unimpressed by the way he had not reported what he saw.

He still felt miserable as he walked back to his flat. He heard the sound of a motorcycle just as he reached the Gardener's House and before he went in. He saw Beth, her back to him, watching the motorbike as it drew to a stop. The man leaned the machine on its stand and took off his helmet. His face, even at this distance, was lit up by a wide smile. Beth rushed towards the rider and threw herself into his arms. They held each other in an embrace which Gordon perceived as intimate, that of lovers who had been separated for some time. He turned and went indoors. Now, he thought, he was not only spying on colleagues, he was behaving like a peeping Tom.

The following morning he left the house for the morning run. The large motorbike was still there. It's none of my business, he told himself as he began running on the towpath. Without thinking, he ran upstream as far as the bridge. For once, the exercise had not cheered him up. He was thinking about Beth's visitor. He had obviously stayed the night. Gordon was strangely upset. He had not considered Beth had a lover, and, if she had, he had no reason to feel jealous. His own relationship with Beth was entirely platonic. His discomfiture arose from his feeling friendless. The daily run was the only part of the day when he could hold a conversation, when everyone, or nearly everyone on the school site was at best wary, at worst hostile and suspicious. The murderer was still among them. The police, whose official duty was to remain apart from the residents, had to maintain a cautious observation as they searched for clues. The residents were not only wary of the police, they were all unsure who could be trusted. In all this, Beth and her Gran had offered a form of normality.

The future looked even more uncertain than the present. Of all the staff, apart from Beth, only two people seemed open and friendly, Raymond Carpenter and the cook. Everybody was worried about the future as well as the existence of a killer in their midst. They had all be told to stay within call of the police. The mutual distrust bound them together like a gigantic spider's web. Gordon had no one to talk to freely other than Beth. Now it seemed she had her own secrets. Then he suddenly thought he had his own private anxieties and guilt, something he had not mentioned to Beth. The thought brought him literally to a halt, just as he was approaching Greenacres. He swore out loud. The situation was a nightmare. The motorbike started up. By the time Gordon was able to see the buildings across the field, the sound was already fading, but he could see Beth, her back to him as she watched the motorbike go. She was waving goodbye. Then she returned in the direction of her flat at the other end of the main building.

He showered, changed and ate breakfast before going to the entrance hall to check the notices. His name featured on police notepaper.

"Will Mr Drake please call on Chief Inspector Blundell as soon s possible."

Gordon thought there should have been a question mark, then realized he was in a mood to find fault. He wanted to be alone – no, he didn't, he wanted to be out of here, surrounded by friends. But he had few friends, he told himself. As the cricket tour neared its end, and he had been distracted by thoughts of Sandra and of his own behaviour, the camaraderie of his team-mates had become tasteless and superficial. His own behaviour had changed. He had suddenly outgrown them This is what parenthood meant, was it? He had kept the secret to himself, but his guilt had cut him off. In Beth he had found a good friend who accepted him as he was, but she did not know him. It was only just that she should have her own secrets.

"Sit down," the big man said.

Gordon did so and looked at him. The Bear had a file in front of him. "I've been looking at the statement you gave to Sergeant Rawlings," he said. "Can you explain what you were doing outside the Beauchamps' house?"

Gordon explained, stammering a little. He was embarrassed, having to explain how he had been spying on a neighbour.

The Bear listened without comment, then asked him to describe in more detail the nature of the files he had seen loaded into the large vehicle. He also asked him to go over what he had seen of the women and children that had boarded the van. But Gordon could add very little.

The Bear frowned and looked at the statement in front of him

"Have you told anyone else about this?" he asked.

"No. I've had other things on my mind," Gordon said.

"Other things? Didn't you think this was all very strange?"

"Well, yes, I suppose so, but I was thinking more about Miss Shepherd."

"Miss Shepherd? Where does she come into the story?"

"She doesn't. But I've been helping her since her grandmother dies."

"I see."

No, you don't, Gordon thought.

"I shall have to take your word for it that you haven't told anyone about all this, not even Miss Shepherd?"

Gordon shook his head.

"Keep it that way," said The Bear. "Leave it to us to do the investigating in future."

"You think this has something to do with the accident?"

"I doubt it, but it's our business, not yours. Did it not occur to you that prowling about in the dark could be dangerous? There is still someone out there who has caused the death of your headmaster."

"I suppose so."

"Show more sense in future, but above all keep your mouth shut. If you remember anything else, tell Sergeant Rawlings, no one else."

Gordon stared the big man in the face. He looked weary. No doubt he was under pressure, too. He got up and left.

Back in the hall, he looked in his pigeon-hole. It was too early to expect further letters from the solicitor but there was a plain envelope. It was a note from Beth.

"Sorry, I'll have to miss the run tomorrow. Something has come up." It was dated the previous day, probably put there late in the day.

Chapter six

Irma Beauchamp looked both apprehensive and defiant as she answered The Bear's demand to report to him in person. She shut the door without any kind of greeting and strode to the chair opposite the Chief Inspector.

"I hope this won't take long," she said. "Your investigation has created a huge amount of extra work. We still have a lot of parents to contact/"

The Bear glared at her. "From what I have seen," he said, "the parents would do well to save their money. They should send their offspring to the new Comprehensive."

"Really!" Irma was outraged.

"Yes, really. Now, I need answers to my questions, not prevarication."

She did not reply to that, but stared at him, uncomprehending.

"I asked you for the personal files of the staff," he said.

"Yes, and I've given them to you."

"There are no files for yourself or your husband."

"Of course not."

"Of course? Why not?"

"It would be very strange for me to draw up a file for myself."

"I can't think why not."

"It would be just – wrong."

"Rubbish! I need that information. I need to know everything about your recruitment and appointment. I would also like to know how you and your husband were employed together. That must surely be unusual."

"I don't see why, but the Governors appointed us. You need to ask them."

"Oh, I shall, I shall. But first, it will save me time if you give me a few facts. You were first appointed five years ago, is that so?"

"Yes."

"And how did you hear about the vacancy?"

"My employer told me about it."

"Your employer? Isn't that unusual?"

"Why should it be?"

"Did he want to get rid of you?"

There was a flash of anger at that. "Of course not!" she said.

"What were you doing and who was this kind boss with your welfare in mind?"

"I was Personnel Manager for Bradshaw's Assurance," she said. "Joseph Bradshaw was one of the senior partners. He told me about the job at Greenacres."

"You say he didn't want to get rid of you?"

"No! Mr Bradshaw is one of the school governors. He knew the secretary was planning to leave and he thought well of my work."

"And your husband?"

"What about my husband?"

"It's obviously not a coincidence that you came here to work at the same time."

"But we didn't."

"You didn't?"

"The Bursar who was in post when I arrived was not very good at the job. He was incompetent. We – we clashed."

"Is that why he left?"

Irma frowned. "I suppose it helped," she said.

"And you saw this as an opening for your husband?"

"It wasn't like that. The school couldn't function without someone to look after the finances. They are surprisingly complicated. Greenacres was a long-established organisation with a lot of staff. We are a registered charity, but we are financially linked with the commercial bakery business. The buildings are quite big and the staff who occupy parts of the property pay rent…Need I go on?"

"I get the picture," The Bear said. "You haven't told me how your husband was recruited. Was that down to you?"

"No. Frank was working as an actuary for another insurance company. He even joked it was a dead-end job. He was looking for another opportunity. I did mention him to Mr Bradshaw, so I suppose I was partly responsible."

"So," The Bear summed up, "this Joseph Bradshaw, a governor, recruited you and recruited your husband shortly afterwards, about six months later."

"And since then you have both been closely concerned with the administration of Greenacres."

"That's right."

"You didn't exactly do a good job."

"What do you mean?"

"Something has been going wrong for some time. Student numbers have been falling. According to Sir Lionel, the school is on the verge of bankruptcy."

"You can't blame us for that," Irma said, but her indignation was tempered by recognition of the problems. "We have both worked hard, but perhaps the school had become outdated. It needed change. That's why the Governors appointed Mr Mulcaster."

"And now your problems are a thousand times worse," The Bear commented without pity. "Who do you think killed him?"

The question shocked her. "I haven't the faintest idea," she said.

"Is there anyone so committed to the status quo they would go to extreme lengths to stop radical change?"

It was such a novel thought that Irma did not reply. She stared at this big, barely civil man and shook her head.

"Now," he said briskly, "I don't care what you are doing at present. I want you to drop everything and to open personal files for yourself and your husband. They will be modelled on the files you have given me for other members of staff, including copies of any correspondence relating to your employment. Just one thing before you start; send your husband in to see me."

"But -we are still dealing with parents –"

"Delegate. This takes absolute priority."

Irma was dismayed but she could not refuse. She left without another word.

The Bear waited a few minutes for the Bursar to arrive. He was picturing to himself the angry conversation taking place next door. He smiled. If Frank Beauchamp was even partly rattled, he could be more likely to drop his guard. For The Bear recognised the Bursar's demeanour as reserved and possibly presenting a shield, hiding something. What that something was, The Bear would like to discover. It might have little or nothing to do with the murder enquiry, but, if that became clearer, the investigation he had already requested into the financial administration of Greenacres could be left to someone else.

"Sit down, Mr Beauchamp," The Bear said.

"I hope this is not going to take long," said the Bursar, "we are very busy phoning parents still. It is not a very agreeable job, but they need to be informed as quickly as possible."

"As I told your wife, you can delegate that task to someone else, if necessary. A police investigation comes first, especially when we're talking about murder."

Beauchamp was startled by the response. "I can't tell you anything about Mr Mulcaster's death," he said. "I've already made a statement, like everyone else."

"Mr Beauchamp," The Bear interrupted him, "you have been far from helpful, as far as I am concerned. As I told your wife, I still have no personal details about you, your previous employment, how and why you were given your present job…"

"But none of this is relevant to your enquiries!"

"That is for me to decide. I have details of all the teaching staff but not of you or Mrs Beauchamp. Not good enough. I asked you to prepare the financial accounts for me. You provided only the sketchiest outline."

"If I gave you the full details," said the Bursar, "you wouldn't understand them. Only a properly trained accountant would be able to make much sense of them." He was staring belligerently at the policeman. The Bear stared back. Beauchamp was tall and thin and the large glasses he wore gave his narrow face an almost comical appearance, but behind the lenses the pupils were sharply distinct and his expression was intense.

"What makes you think," said The Bear, "that I would be the one to examine the books? We have our own specialists. We also have a fraud squad."

The stare became more intense. "What are you suggesting?" he asked.

"Nothing, Mr Beauchamp, "I haven't any evidence, since you have so far failed to provide it, but there are some strange things going on here that warrant investigation."

"What are you talking about?"

"Can you tell me why you were observed loading files into your campervan in the middle of the night?"

Beauchamp was speechless and obviously shocked by the question.

"And what was in those files?" The Bear continued.

"Have you got your men spying on us?"

"Answer the question."

"I was appointed to this post nearly five years ago," said Beauchamp. He was angry. The words came from a mouth that was tense, the tendons in his neck and lower jaw stood out under the skin. "The man before me was completely hopeless. We are obliged by law to keep financial records six years. With my wife's help I sorted out all the old records up to 1954, the year before I took over. The old records were virtually unintelligible, so we put all but the last year's files in cardboard boxes and cleared them out of the office."

"To your house?"

"Yes, temporarily."

"And that is what you were taking away?"

"Yes. I wanted to make sure they were properly destroyed and the Council has a special furnace for destroying confidential documents."

"In the middle of the night?"

"I realise it sounds strange, but in fact, although it's true we loaded them in the van overnight, I only took them to the furnace first thing in the morning."

"Even you must agree this sounds unusual."

"Maybe."

"I can't think of many married couples who would go out in the small hours of the morning to clear out office papers."

"There's nothing illegal in that."

"If you say so." Beauchamp was still returning The Bear's gaze, but he did not reply.

"You seem to make a habit of it," The Bear added.

"What do you mean?"

"You took your van across the wet grass as far as the main entrance," said The Bear. The thin figure looked even more rigid.

"What?"

"You were seen driving from your house. You stopped long enough to pick up two women and several small children from the school building. You then drove off towards the main road."

"Have you been keeping me under observation? This is an invasion of my privacy!"

"I hope you aren't denying this?"

"No, it's true enough, but who has been spying on us and why?"

"No one is spying, Mr Beauchamp. The information comes from statements."

"But who?"

"I can't tell you that. I want you to explain what you were up to, taking these people away in the night again."

Beauchamp said nothing for a while. The Bear watched as consternation gave way slowly to indignation.

"The people you were referring to," he said at last, "were two Punjabi women and their children. They had been staying here with other family members until they moved on to Nottingham."

"Nottingham! You didn't drive them to Nottingham?"

"No, only as far as Horsham. Another member of the family drove as far as Horsham to pick them up."

"Why the secrecy? Why in the night?"

"It was the only time the man could get away to drive here. His family runs a small shop that is open all hours."

"And how did you get involved?"

Beauchamp heaved an impatient sigh. "It's a long story," he said, "and it has nothing to do with Mulcaster's accident."

"You keep telling me none of this is my business," said The Bear, his expression becoming hostile and irritated. "I am the one to decide what is and what isn't relevant. So far you have told me a string of barely credible explanations of frankly bizarre behaviour. I shall, of course, check out as much as I can. So far, I have only your word for it that these two nocturnal adventured were innocent. I shall ask you to tell Sergeant Rawlings everything you have told me and are now going to tell me. He will take this down as a formal statement for you to sign, together with names and addresses for us to check the details about your burning the documents, and the man you say collected your passengers in Horsham. Meanwhile you can also explain how and why you have come to employ several other Indian people."

Beauchamp looked extremely annoyed.

"It's not that strange," he said. "Ask Ernest Jenkins."

"Who is Ernest Jenkins?"

"He's a Governor."

"What has he got to do with all this"

"He has something to do with that part of India."

"What do you mean, 'something to do with'?"

"I don't know. He just told me some Punjabis that he knew were eager to emigrate to start a new life in England – something about political problems. He said he would vouch for them and they would earn their keep. They weren't afraid of hard work, he said. And they weren't. They've been very good employees."

"What about the women?"

"Well, I didn't exactly expect that. The women came later. They had temporary visas only but hoped to stay on to avoid returning to the Punjab. It would be dangerous for them, according to Mr Jenkins."

The Bear sent him on to Sergeant Rawlings and left his desk in search of a cup of tea. He suspected Beauchamp was right about one thing. This had nothing to do with Mulcaster's death. He was both annoyed and confused at the way the Governors of Greenacres seemed to be intimately involved is different ways. As well as the more obvious, official overseeing of the school, the appointment of Mulcaster was surely irregular, at the personal recommendation of a friend. Sir Lionel had used his position to keep the totally unsuitable Stephen Wilder in post. Another, Joseph Bradshaw, had been very influential, even instrumental, in the appointment of both Beauchamps. Now this Ernest Jenkins was using the school to harbour Punjabi immigrants and their dependents, family members who might well be illegal. The Bear took his mug of tea outside and stood for a few minutes in the cool air, staring at the quiet scene across the grass and across the river. If this establishment was obliged to close, he hoped at least the estate would remain untouched. His distaste, he realised, came from an increasing smell of corruption. There was more to come, he felt sure. He breathed another lungful of fresh, country air, and turned back to the Operations Room.

"WPC Burton?" A young woman looked up as The Bear addressed her by name. She looked almost too pretty to be a policewoman, thought The Bear. Dark, shoulder-length hair framed an oval face. Clear, blue eyes looked at him as she made to stand.

"Don't get up," he said. "How far have you got with reading the minutes?"

"Well," said WPC Burton, "I didn't start at the very beginning because the first Board of Governors met in 1885. I began with meetings held since 1955."

"Sensible idea," The Bear said. "And have you been through the last five years?"

"Yes, sir. I've now gone back a further five years to 1950, but I haven't finished yet."

"Follow me to my office," he ordered. "Bring your notes and the minute books for the last five years."

He returned to his office and waited for her to follow him with the documents in question. She did not take long. She carried two large books. They must either have been left over from years ago or specially made to match earlier volumes. They were foolscap in size, bound in green leather, and embossed with Minutes in gold on the front cover. On the spine of one book, also in gold, was printed Jan 1945 – Aug 1950. The second had only the starting date, Sept 1950 -.

"I brought both books in case you wanted to go back more than five years," she said.

"Before I look at them." The Bear said, as she placed them on his desk, "I want your observations."

"What do you want me to comment on?"

"Anything you have noticed that strikes you as irregular in any way. I take it wrote down your impressions."

"Yes, sir, but I didn't really know what I was looking for. To tell you the truth I still don't know."

"Never mind all that. Tell me what you noticed."

"Well, sir, the first thought was how old-fashioned these records are. They are all written by hand. I would have expected official records to be typed. That way they could be filed easily."

The Bear acknowledged her remarks with a grunt and opened the book in front of him. He opened it at random. The time and date of a meeting was written at the top of a page, followed by a list of those present. The handwriting was legible, but not especially stylish. The Bear was surprised. He knew little about these things, but he had imagined handwritten minutes would look like the fine, copperplate style used in Dickens' day.

"The next thing," said Pearl Burton, "is what seems to be a lack of formality."

"What does that mean?" The discussion seemed to have little to do with his enquiry, but it was unusual enough to be oddly refreshing. And he was for once enjoying sharing his office with an attractive young woman.

"I would have expected the meetings to follow an agenda, prepared in advance and each item to be voted on."

"But motions are recorded, surely?"

"Yes, but it reads like they made them up among themselves, and most of them seem to be giving approval for actions already taken."

"I'm not sure I follow you. Give me an example."

"OK." Pearl flipped the pages of her notebook. "August 1956 – the minutes aren't numbered for reference – I quote : 'Mr Pearson said he had been talking to Messrs Margrove and Co, who said they could provide school uniforms at a reasonable cost, and would pay the school ten percent commission, provided they had the exclusive rights. Mr Pearson reckoned the school should accept this offer. After a short discussion the contract was agreed.' That's the closest the governors got to a formal proposal to adopt a contract."

The Bear nodded. "No open bidding, no invitation to tender for a contract; I see what you mean. I don't think this has a direct relevance to the death of Greenville Mulcaster, however. There are three events which should have involved the governors recently, and another that is buried further in the past.

"Firstly, is there any recent reference to the departure of the groundsman? Secondly, was there any reference made to the state of health of the previous headmaster? Thirdly, what discussion took place, leading to the appointment of Mulcaster? Weren't the governors beginning to panic about the school's future? Finally, have you found any direct references or discussion about Stephen Wilder?"

"I don't know what you hope to find, sir, but the informal style of these minutes leaves everything vague. "

"Vague?"

"It's almost as though the writer is avoiding too much detail. I did notice two or three references to Mr Wilder. It seems he had to spend two lengthy periods in hospital somewhere. The reason is not stated. There was also a complaint lodged against him, but the details are not given and the Chairman, Sir Lionel, appears to have defended him, but no details."

"Right, thank you, Constable."

"Do you want to hang on to the minute books, sir?"

"No. I'd like you to carry on. Make sure you keep your notes up to date. If you can, identify those governors whose decisions have had any consequences for the school. Do I understand that the Bursar submitted a financial report for each occasion?"

"Yes, sir, but they are only referred to in the minute books and are kept on typewritten sheets in a separate file."

"Can you understand balance sheets?"

"These seem plain enough, but they are a bit like the minutes."

"How?"

"They have too many general categories, like 'sundry office supplies' and even 'Stagg insurances'"

"For the moment, make notes about them too. We need someone with the financial expertise to look at them."

"Wasn't that what the new headmaster was good at?"

The Bear sat motionless and stared at her until she wondered what she had said wrong. To hide her confusion she stood up and collected the books from the desk.

"Thank you," said The Bear. "Well done."

She had no idea what she had done other than the obvious. She had uncovered no secrets. Instead, she had reported what she had found, pages of boring, handwritten records that obscured the past rather than clarifying it.

"OK, Pearl?" asked Sergeant Rawlings as she returned.

"Yes, thank you, Sarge. He seemed satisfied, even thanked me."

"You must have done well, then," the sergeant said, and went to the door.

"Come in, Sergeant."

"A small success, sir. We managed to track down the groundsman."

"Well done. I'm glad of any positive results. This case is too complicated. All I want to do is find the person who cut the brake pipes on Mulcaster's car. Instead, I'm being led all over the place into maladministration, possibly fraud."

"Fraud, sir?"

"I don't know, maybe not, but things seem very complicated. We have opened a real can of worms this time."

"So, is it a can of worms or a nest of vipers?"

The Bear grinned. It was a rare event, like the disappearance of the moon's shadow at the end of an eclipse.

"Right," said the big man, "what did the groundsman have to say?"

"It sounds pretty reasonable," Rawlings said, "Or it would if you didn't have Pearl Burton on the case."

"Pearl Burton? What has she got to do with this? I thought it was Jackson you had on the job."

"That's right, but Pearl also checked out the bit in the Governors' minutes as reported by Frank Beauchamp. The accounts don't exactly match."

"How?"

"The groundsman, Groom, says he was sacked. A week earlier, he says, his daughter, who is a primary school teacher, happened to mention how she had to pay four percent of her salary into the compulsory pension fund. Groom said he was paying six percent, and he thought that was a bit steep. So, he spoke to one of the junior teachers (he has since left) and discovered the teachers seemed to be paying six percent. He took it up with the Bursar, who told him the staff here are enrolled in a private scheme with other benefits. But then Groom was called into the office two days later, told his services were no longer required, and given a golden handshake of eight hundred pounds."

"It does sound a bit strange," The Bear agreed.

"Yes, but quite plausible, except for Beauchamp's report to the governors. According to the minutes, he reported that Groom had given in his notice late, saying he had been offered a job in the new garden centre. In view of his long service, the Bursar had paid him the eight hundred pounds bonus."

"It all sounds irregular," The Bear conceded, "but nothing very relevant to our enquiry. I'm asking for someone with financial know-how to come and look through the school accounts. We can't afford to be distracted from our main suspects."

"I get that, boss, but Grenville Mulcaster was a trained accountant. He would surely have been likely to sniff out any financial irregularities."

The Bear look at the Sergeant musingly. "You've got a point," he said. "I'm still inclined to think it's a red herring. We'll wait and see what our new colleague discovers. It would surely need to be a lot more serious than cheating the Exchequer of a few pounds by using a private insurance company." He tapped his fingers together, then, struck by a different idea, added, "I wonder if, by any chance, the insurance is with Bradshaw's."

Rawlings looked at him, not comprehending the significance.

"As I said," The Bear concluded, "we'll leave it to the Fraud Squad, or whoever the Super sends."

Chapter seven

Although the morning runs continued, something had changed. Now he knew of Beth's boyfriend, he recognized he, Gordon, had come to depend on Beth far too much. He had only known her a short time, and had not considered that she had her own life outside the school. It was unfair to depend so heavily on her as his sole friend. It was also quite probably not healthy for him. It was fine to team up with her for the morning run, but anything more could be inappropriate.

Beth too was conscious of the change. Gordon talked less. She assumed it was to do with her grandmother's death. Gordon had hardly known her, having met her once, but he had been kind and understanding at the hospital and during the first, awful hours. He had been kind to look after the cats, too. She ascribed his new coolness to a sensitive reaction to her grief. He was a very nice man.

They greeted one another almost formally, then one or other would begin to run. It was Gordon who took the lead first, setting off downstream, not pausing to look for traces of badgers. When they reached the gate to the meadow, he stopped long enough to catch his breath before asking, "OK?" Beth nodded, and they set off on the return run. Back at the games field, Gordon continued as far as the buildings, turned, said, "'Bye. Thank you," and headed for the Gardener's House.

Beth was just a little puzzled by this behaviour. She liked Gordon, was ready to get to know him better, but his consideration for her was an obstacle. Perhaps things would return to normal once the funeral was over. With that thought she turned her attention to all the business involved in talking to the solicitor who was the co-executor of her grandmother's will. The cottage had already been valued. The contents were worth little, but she had to sort them, following the solicitor's instructions.

The uncertainty felt by the entire staff meant that everyone was on the watch for signs. That involved consulting the notice boards every day, looking to see whose names came up on the police lists, but also watching for information posted by Harold Black or by Irma Beauchamp. One such notice appeared, but its meaning and importance were obscure. The Assembly Hall would be out of bounds all day on Friday afternoon, the School Secretary announced. There was to be a Governors' meeting. No further details were given, but Harold Black had added "The Governors are aware of the anxiety about the future of Greenacres. They will be calling a full meeting of the staff on Saturday, when Sir Lionel will try to make the situation clear and had agreed to answer any questions."

This merely increased the uncertainty, and Harold refused to answer any questions until Saturday.

Other senior members of staff would say nothing either, whether because they knew nothing or because they were following agreed policy. Consequently, rumours abounded. The optimists said there would be a new headmaster appointed after Friday, perhaps Harold Black. The pessimists said the Governors would announce redundancies, perhaps to take immediate effect. The most pessimistic of all forecast the school would be run down over the year and faced closure the following summer. The senior staff who had been chiefly involved in telephoning parents all looked consistently stressed, reinforcing the earliest rumours about parents wanting to withdraw their boys.

At eleven o'clock on Friday morning the Governors arrived for their meeting. The drive was soon lined with large, expensive cars. Teachers, trying to look casual, wandered about the entrance hall and corridors. The staffroom, mostly deserted in the holidays, was unusually busy. The air inside was blue with cigarette smoke.

Gordon was uneasy and restless, but he needed to be outside. He went back to the river and watched the wildlife, trying to spot fish. Then he walked back to where he and Beth had run that morning and he began looking to see what birds he could find. He thought he could distinguish six species, though he did not know their names. Four kinds of birds swam on the river. He thought he could recognise mallards, but not the others. He resolved to get hold of an illustrated book and perhaps a cheap pair of binoculars. Perhaps he should ask Williams for advice.

The day passed slowly. The meeting broke up at three o'clock and the sound of engines filled the drive. The cars turned, driving over the grass, sending little clouds of smoke across the meadow and leaving the smell behind as they drove into the traffic on the main road.

Inside, few of the senior staff were to be seen. Those that were, shook their heads when asked direct questions. They all looked grim, unsmiling.

Six days after Mulcaster had addressed the assembled staff, Gordon once more took his seat in the Assembly Hall together with the rest of the staff. This time there was little talking. That had filled the past twenty-four hours. The atmosphere was febrile.

The swing doors opened and five people came in and took their places at the front. Gordon was able to identify four of them. Sir Lionel Beckingham sat in the middle of the row. On his left sat Harold Black. Next to Harold, Irma Beauchamp clutched a notebook. On the other side of the Chairman was a man Gordon had not seen before, and the next seat was taken by DCI Blundell.

Sir Lionel wasted no time. There was no stylish introduction by the Acting Headmaster. Sir Lionel greeted everyone briefly and named the other four. The mystery man was named as Simon Prendergast, solicitor. The reason for his attendance would become clear, said Sir Lionel. He was the legal consultant who advised the Board on legal matters.

"This past week," Sir Lionel Began, "has been distressing for all of us. Less than a week ago we faced a crisis. The Governors hoped the appointment of Grenville Mulcaster might prevent the decline of Greenacres. Falling numbers plus competition from the new comprehensive school were threatening the very future of the school. The tragic circumstances of Mulcaster's death you all know about. The police investigation, led by Detective Chief Inspector Blundell, had consequences we could not have foreseen. Senior members of staff have spent many hours making personal contact with individual parents. We, the Govternors, had no option but to postpone the opening of term. That, and the unease created by the investigation itself, achieved the opposite effect to that we hoped would result from Mr Mulcaster's appointment. Of the two hundred parents, forty-one have told us their sons will not be returning."

This provoked a reaction and a great deal of talking. Sir Lionel leaned on his stick and waited for the noise to subside.

"I need hardly tell you", he said, "that the resulting twenty percent reduction in income from fees would be unviable. Greenacres School is non-profit making, but it is expected not to run at a loss. Our hands are tied. We have informed the Charity Commissioners of the situation and of our intention to wind up the business."

There was more, noisy conversation at this. A lone voice cried, "Where's Frank Beauchamp?" Sir Lionel waited again until the hubbub subsided, then answered the question, "Mr Beauchamp is snowed under, preparing statements and provisional budgets. Among other things, we are obliged to deal with our employees fairly. Your contracts will come to an end in two months' time. We, that is the Bursa and the Governors, are trying to recompense you in the form of redundancy payments, if we can find the money."

Sir Lionel was faced with an increasingly hostile audience, but he managed to keep control. His manner was frank and reasonable. He explained the presence of DCI Blundell and the solicitor. The solicitor was ready to explain the situation as it affected all employees. The policeman told them his investigation was far from complete and, even though their contracts were to end shortly, they would be required to remain within reach for now.

Gordon was one of the least affected by the announcement, but he was thinking about looking for another job. He was impressed by Sir Lionel who remained calm amidst all the anger and dismay and the underlying sense of betrayal. He invited questions. There was no hiding the anger with which they were addressed , especially since the Chairman repeated many times that details would not be available for some time. The DCI said his piece, then asked the Chairman to excuse him, and left. Gordon decided to follow suit, as did half a dozen others. One of them was Beth.

There was coffee available in the entrance hall. Everyone seemed to be in need of something to counteract dejection, but they stood, nursing their cups in silence.

Gordon turned to Beth. "What are you going to do?" he asked.

"About a job?"

"Yes."

"I've no idea, not until after the funeral."

He should have thought. "Of course," he said.

"I have to sort out the cottage and deal with the solicitor. I'll worry about a new job after that."

Gordon, over-sensitive, took this as a snub. He fell silent.

"What about you?" Beth asked.

"I'll start looking round," he said. "I don't think I'll be looking for teaching jobs, though. I don't know what I want to do, but I do need to get a job. I have commitments."

She looked at him then, expecting him to explain, but he didn't. The Sandra business was still raw.

"I don't want to hang around here," he said. "I thought I might drive into town and look in the Job Centre. It might give me some ideas."

She nodded, but she did not seem interested. After a little while she put down her cup and left the hall by the main door. She did not say goodbye. Gordon felt lonely. He had been at Greenacres a week, but he had not had time to make friends other than Beth. Now their relationship had turned cool. Perhaps he had imagined it was warmer than it really was. The time he had spent with Beth when her grandmother had been taken ill and died, had been intense, but the circumstances were unusual. The appearance of her boyfriend had come as a surprise, but he now needed to reassess the situation. They shared an interest in keeping fit. That was all.

By now the meeting was breaking up. Small groups of people were drifting disconsolately into the hall. They sipped coffee and talked in subdued tones. The anger and denial expressed in the meeting seemed to have given way to shock and anxiety. While everyone was aware of the accident that had proved to be a planned act of sabotage, many of the staff had not foreseen the grave threat to their employment. It was real now, and they had been told they would each receive a personal letter which would contain formal notice that their job was coming to an end, together with information about the payment (severance payment was the term used) each would be offered. A major concern for most of them was the loss of somewhere to live. Young, unmarried individuals might face a temporary return to the family home. The older, married couples might scrape together the money to rent or buy. Many others faced a difficult time. They had been unable to save much on their modest salary.

Gordon headed for the car park and drove out of the school grounds. It was good to get away, though his mood was not gay. He headed for town. He walked as far as the front and sat for a while, gazing at the sea. The tide was coming in. Each wave washed over the shingle beach, rattling the stones as it retreated with a hissing, sucking noise. The water was grey, matching his mood, but there was something soothing about the regularity of movement and sound. Half-heartedly, he lobbed a few pebbles into the sea. Then he brushed off sand and walked back into town. He found a café and ordered a hot meal. There were not many people about. He sat by a window and watched as he ate.

There were several cafes here, as was common in seaside towns. On the other side of the street, two or three doors down, was another eating place. As Gordon ate his chicken curry, he saw Beth. She was on the arm of a good-looking man and laughed up at him. Gordon was quite sure it was the man with the motorbike. He was embarrassed. Once again he had the feeling he was spying on them. Just before they went into the café, Beth took he hand from the man's arm in order to embrace him, then she reached up and kissed him on the cheek. He remembered how she had kissed him when she got out of his car. He felt jealous and told himself not to be silly. When left a short time later, he hurried down the street away from the café where Beth was with her boyfriend and took pains to look down and away from that side of the street.

He found the Job Centre. He had never been inside a job centre before. There were three desks where people were ready to deal with queries. There were also several large notice boards on which cards were pinned, advertising vacancies for a surprizing variety of occupations. There was, I seemed, a dearth of carers to look after elderly people in residential homes. Many vacancies demanded specific skills – experienced
cooks and chefs, a quantity surveyor, an experienced printer, even a mechanical engineer with experience in industrial manufacturing, several financial executives. He gave up without speaking to an assistant and was walking back to his car when he passed a camera shop. He ignored the expensive camera equipment because at the bottom of the window there were second-hand bargains. Among them was a pair of binoculars. He went in and bought them on impulse, then he returned to the main street and entered a bookshop. Half an hour later he was heading for his car again. He

paused long enough to buy a local paper. He would look at the 'Jobs Vacant' page later.

He felt better when he got back to his flat. He strolled down to the river and spent a while observing the waterfowl. With the aid of his new book, he identified shelduck, goldeneye, pochard and a little moorhen which scuttled away under cover. He would need to think of some way to keep the pages dry, he realized. It would also be harder to identify the small birds in the trees or even on the ground, but it was a pleasant way to pass the time.

He was engrossed in all this and did not notice Mr Williams until he was close by.

"You got yourself some glasses, then?" the older man observed.

"Yes, saw them in the shop window, second hand."

Williams held out his hand and examined them. "They'll be fine," he said.

"I've no idea really. I bought a book, too."

"Ah! That's important. What are the illustrations like?"

"Not very lifelike," Gordon said, "almost like cartoons in some ways, but they are very clear." He handed the book to Williams.

"Another good choice," said the other man ."What they point out is the colour of the plumage in the various areas, breast, back, wings, top and underside, and, very important, length and shape of the beak and the legs."

"I've got a lot to learn," Gordon admitted.

"Why don't you come out with me? I can give you a few tips."

"That would be good, but I imagine half the pleasure is being on your own."

"Of course, you are right. I wouldn't want to chatter. The essential thing is to observe without disturbing the birds or any other wildlife."

"Other wildlife?"

"Get up really early, say five o'clock, and you might see the badgers. And I have seen a few deer in the meadows."

So began an unexpected, new friendship. Williams ("Call me Aled," he said) was happy to share his enthusiasm and interest provided talking was kept to a minimum. Early morning expeditions often concluded after dawn in time for Gordon to join Beth on a run. But not all the nature walks were in the early morning. Some were at twilight or even later, and Aled Williams introduced Gordon to the soundless, ghostly flights of barn owls, hunting their prey in the grass. There was more wildlife than Gordon had expected, including game birds, mostly pheasants and some inconspicuous partridges. They spent one cold, misty morning with the badgers. ("I know it's cheating," said Aled, scattering a tin of dog food on the bare ground.) For the first time in his life one morning Gordon watched three roe deer cross the meadow, away from the cows. The athlete in him found their graceful, elegant, effortless movement breathtakingly beautiful.

"I wish I'd had a camera," he said, as the two men returned to Greenacres at six o'clock, their breath forming little clouds. Gordon had come to realize, too, that what he had thought of as silence was full of birdsong. Aled seemed able to identify the birds by their calls, a skill Gordon knew would take a long time to learn.

Conversation was minimal, so it was a while before Gordon learned much about the Welshman. It was not appropriate to ask personal questions. Information dropped accidentally, like crumbs from a sandwich. Williams carried a large pair of field glasses round his neck. Gordon commented on their size.

"Oh, these? Too heavy, really, but very good optically. I had them in the army, so I grew used to them."

"Someone said you were a soldier."

"One of the lucky ones. I was wounded in '42."

"And that was lucky?"

"I was reassigned to a training job after that."

"But I was told you won medals!"

Williams looked at him, surprised. "That's when I was sent home," he said.

The conversation moved back to birds, and it was some days before the army was mentioned again. On that occasion Gordon happened to mention Stephen Wilder who, he said, 'seemed to have had a bad war'.

"Yes, poor chap," Williams said. "I don't think he'll ever get over it. I try to talk to him, but we don't have much in common except the school, and he's not exactly dedicated to teaching. The war is taboo."

Although he checked the notice boards every day, there was nothing new. The police seemed to have settled in permanently. Indeed, their number grew. A uniformed officer with pips on his shoulders moved in to share the headmaster's office with the DCI. There was no formal announcement of who he was or why he had arrived, but Gordon noticed that his arrival was followed by a succession of people who were shut in with the two policemen in a series of consultations or interviews. One of the first was Sir Lionel. Gordon thought one or two of the others were familiar. Several days passed without the Wanted List containing any teachers' names. There must be a new line of enquiry.

Chapter eight

The new line of enquiry was initiated at The Bear's request. None of the evidence so far pointed unequivocally towards an identifiable suspect, but inconsistencies and observations suggested something strange was going on in Greenacres. One peculiarity was the appearance and departure of the Punjabi women and children. Another was the Bursar's destruction of official records in the middle of the night. The sacking of the groundsman still seemed questionable. The generally poor management by the Governors, as picked up by WPC Butler was strangely suspect, too, given the situation.

The Bear could see no obvious connection between all this and the death of Grenville Mulcaster. He had the uneasy feeling that there were financial irregularities, especially in view of the general lack of cooperation on the part of the Bursar. He had reluctantly said as much to the Superintendent with the result he expected but half feared, and DCI Carghill arrived. He was of lower rank than The Bear, but he had special experience and skill in financial investigations. He was a qualified accountant with a knowledge of the law and of Company

Law in particular. Fortunately, he was also modest, and The Bear found him good to work with.

The Bear handed over the pile of ledgers and files he had at last received from Frank Beauchamp, and Carghill looked briefly at the titles and headings.

"Right," he said, "I'll take a quick look at these today and get back to you. Do you know if the Governors kept their own accounts?"

"Beauchamp did it all, so far as I can tell," said The Bear. "He submitted a report each time they met."

"Who are the auditors?"

"I think they are named in the report of the AGM."

"Good. Thank you, sir. I'll tell you what I find, if anything, tomorrow." With that, to The Bear's surprise, Carghill took his seat at the desk which had been set up at the opposite side of the headmaster's office and put the ledgers in three neat piles next to a small tape-recorder. He donned a pair of earphones and turned on the recorder while he worked.

The Bear pointed at the machine and made an enquiring face. Carghill pressed a button and eased the earphones from his ears.

"I assumed you wouldn't mind, sir," he said. "It helps me concentrate. Classical music. You can't hear it, can you?"

The Bear shook his head as much in wonder as to answer the question. Sharing the office was his idea. His own enquiries had reached a point where he saw no way further. He hoped the financial investigation might produce a lead. He hoped it would clear a lot of strange doubts out of the way. Meanwhile, he was able to watch Carghill, stay in close touch as he sorted the muddle. If he chose to clamp the headphones to his ears and resemble a robot, at least he would work silently.

In any case he was free to leave the school to visit some of the governors. Carghill told him on the second day that he wanted to speak to the Bursar. There were a number of peculiarities which only Beauchamp could explain.

"Peculiarities?"

"Yes, sir, things like the confidentiality clause in the employment contracts. Why are the employees asked or even ordered not to discuss their contracts? I see the insurance scheme is compulsory, which means that the teachers are compelled to withdraw from the national Teachers' Pension Scheme. I want to know how the school benefits. Several things like that."

"You think there's something fishy going on?"

"No question about that. Take just one case: why is the English teacher, Williams, paid well over the odds? A note in the ledger says it is on the specific instructions of Sir Lionel."

"How much over the odds?"

"An extra five hundred pounds a year."

The Bear's eyebrows shot up. "Any other members of staff getting special treatment?"

"Not that I can see so far."

The Bear said nothing more, but he left the office in search of Aled Williams. The teacher was not in his flat, however. He made his way to the general office in the hope Irma Beauchamp might know where her could find the man.

"Why should I know where he is? Her tone was sharply hostile now.

"I merely hoped…"

"He's probably wandering the grounds somewhere. He's a keen birdwatcher." She turned her attention to papers on her desk. The Bear left without thanking her, aware that Frank Beauchamp was watching him.

He decided to walk as far as the river, leaving his colleague to continue digging in the financial files. It was a good excuse to escape the confines of four walls. At the river's edge he gazed round, then walked the short distance to the groundsman's hut where he found a convenient log to sit on. A few ducks swam here and there, the only sign of life. The only sound was birdsong. He had not noticed it before. He was deliberately trying to empty his mind, to let all the curious and seemingly disjointed information settle like silt in a disturbed lake.

"Hello, Chief Inspector!" A strong voice called from the pathway on his left.

"Mr Williams!"

"Come to admire the ducks, have you?"

"No. In fact I've been looking for you."

"Oh? And someone told you I like it down here by the river?"

"No, I just happened to be down here."

"Well, it's a nice place to be. What do you want to ask me about?"

Williams was supremely relaxed. He was, The Bear thought, ready to hold a conversation as though he had nothing to hide. Very few people in The Bear's experience, could honestly claim they had no secrets.

"Would you prefer it if I spoke to you in the office?"

Williams looked surprised at that. "Ask away", he said. "I can't imagine what it is you want to know that's so important."

"Your salary," said The Bear.

"My salary? What about it?"

"It's remarkably good."

"Is it? I'm not sure how it compares with the rest of the teaching staff. As Head of Department, I'd expect a decent allowance above the basic."

"But you have an exceptionally high allowance and according to the confidential accounts, the allowance was awarded at the personal request of Sir Lionel Beckingham."

"I suppose that is quite unusual."

"I should think so. Can you explain it? What is the special relationship you have with him? Have you got some kind of hold over him,?"

Williams looked astonished. He stared at the policeman for a moment without responding, then he gave a curious laugh. "Are you suggesting I am blackmailing the Chairman of the Governors?" The incredulous laugh turned into loud, genuine laughter. "Don't be ridiculous!" he said at last.

"Then why? How?"

Still relaxed, Williams sat down on the large log outside the groundsman's hut. "Well," he said, "the information is confidential but not in the least sinister. I'm sure you won't want to spread it round?"

The Bear did not reply one way or the other.

"When I was first appointed to the job," Williams explained, "Sir Lionel was eager to ask me about my war service. I wasn't too keen to tell him much. I prefer to put it behind me. But then he took me into his confidence and told me that young Stephen Winter was his godson. It was obvious on first sight that Stephen had – well, let's say problems."

"He's an alcoholic," said The Bear.

Williams appeared to find such bluntness offensive. He nodded. "Among other things," he said.

"Go on."

"I take a more compassionate view of such matters than you, it seems." The Bear said nothing.

"He had a rough time," said Williams. "Sir Lionel wanted to protect him, help him. He even paid for the poor chap to spend time in a private clinic. I believe he has recently given him an ultimatum."

"Where does your salary come into this sad, little story?"

Williams gave The Bear a withering stare. He was angered by the big man's lack of compassion. His tone changed. He spoke with the firm voice of a man used to giving commands and being obeyed without question. "Sir Lionel asked me to keep an eye on his godson, befriend him if possible."

"If possible?"

"It was difficult. This is a young man who has been through hell and who experienced a mental breakdown. For a long time he trusted no one. After his second course of treatment…"

"He dried out?"

"Not for long, but he was virtually suicidal at times. He reacted by allowing himself to give up most of his self-discipline, especially when drunk."

"And that would be most of the time?"

"Yes, a great deal of the time."

"So, your work as a paid befriender wasn't much help"

"No – and I did not like the arrangement. I certainly felt sorry for both Stephen and Sir Lionel, but I could not help. In fact, I may have made matters worse recently."

"How?"

"As I said, I prefer not to talk much about the war, but I do attend a regimental reunion once a year."

"And?"

"An old friend and I were chatting casually over a drink in August at the last reunion dinner. Unlike me, he tends to enjoy reminiscing. He, too, spent time in Intelligence and an unexpected coincidence was revealed. By chance, I mentioned we were about to get a new headmaster, and I mentioned his name, Mulcaster. My colleague was surprised at the name. He asked one or two questions and identified him as a former officer in Intelligence who was responsible for a dreadful blunder. Although I didn't tell him, I realized this was the same man who had authorized Stephen Wilder's doomed attack on the chateau in France. Then I did the unforgivably stupid thing. I told Sir Lionel."

"And he still went ahead and employed the man?"

"It was too late to withdraw."

The Bear was staring intently at the landscape.

"Think carefully," he said. "Do you know if Sir Lionel passed on the information to Stephen Welder?"

"I don't know," said Williams. "If he did, it would have done nothing to help calm

Stephen's troubled mind. He would surely have known that."

"But if he did," said The Bear,"you can see where this leads."

"Stephen isn't capable of murder," said Williams, "especially if it requires planning and mechanical dexterity. He has the shakes."

"And Sir Lionel?"

Williams did not reply. He shrugged, aware of and horrified by his own, thoughtless part in all this. After a few minutes' silence, he stood up and strode off towards the school. The Bear watched him, a small figure but ramrod erect.

Chapter nine

Gordon showered and dressed after the morning run. He was beginning to regret the agreement to run with Beth. It felt increasingly awkward. What had begun as an uncomplicated sharing of a simple pleasure was now inexplicably infused with complicated emotion. He was attracted to Beth in a way he found inconvenient. The last thing he wanted was a romantic entanglement. The pleasure he had taken from sharing this physical activity had its origins in a purely platonic companionship. His growing recognition of the new, sexual element was disturbing, inconvenient and it tended to detract from the pleasure of running. He did not know how to get out of the arrangement. Beth's behaviour seemed to have changed, too. She said very little, but he wondered if it was his own taciturnity which caused her to change. Perhaps she was more aloof so as not to encourage a closer connection. She might be acting from a concern for her relationship with her boyfriend. Yet Gordon also wished he could develop a deeper friendship. He wanted someone to talk to. At first Beth had seemed ideal in that respect, but not now.

He ate a bowl of cereal, rinsed the bowl, and left the flat. It had become a routine to check the notices in the entrance hall. He headed that way, noting that the campervan was no longer parked outside the Steward's House. Frank Beauchamp must have urgent business to attend to in town. It was still only eight o'clock.

He looked at the notices; no one wanted to see him. He checked the pigeonholes without expecting any post unless his parents had written. There was a letter for him, but one glance was enough to tell him it was from the solicitors. What now, he wondered. They could surely not want him to pay more maintenance. His confused mind clouded over with resentment, anxiety and guilt. He still had no idea what employment he could find. With a leaden heart he told himself he must make a serious effort to look for a new job. Perhaps he might at least find seasonal work, since his employment here ended at the end of November. Yes, a month or so working in a hotel somewhere could provide accommodation as well as an income until he could think more clearly. The thought cheered him a little. He had made some sort of a decision.

It was cool but dry outside. He left the hall and found a sheltered, grassy bank overlooking the field in front of the school. The grass was growing again and looked untidy. He would get out the tractor today and tidy it up. It would give him something to do.

He opened the letter. Why did solicitors always use bigger envelopes and write their letters on paper bigger than foolscap? He read the first lines without taking them in and was obliged to re-read them.

"Dear Mr Drake," he read, "We are writing to inform you that the agreement you have signed with respect of maintenance payments to Miss Sandra Embury is herewith cancelled. Miss Embury's miscarriage means such an agreement is no longer needed or appropriate. There are some, minor expenses resulting from this unfortunate event, and you may feel it appropriate to contribute towards them. Miss Embury, however, has expressly instructed us to tell you she does not want you to contact her in person, and has instructed us to deal with any further, financial contributions or claims. We understand that a one-off payment of one hundred pounds would cover the costs associated with the unhappy end to the pregnancy. If you agree to such a payment, which should be sent by cheque made out to us, the correspondence in this matter will be considered closed. Yours faithfully, "

Gordon was again prey to a range of emotions. The first and most immediate was relief that a huge burden of anxiety had been swept away. He would no longer be faced with a long-term drain on his income. But no sooner had this thought struck him than another, very familiar sense of shame took its place. A miscarriage must be a devastating experience. Sandra had been carrying his child. Irrespective of the unplanned nature of the pregnancy, she had been growing their child inside her. It really was part of her flesh. He had no idea of the physical distress she must be experiencing, but he could at least begin to imagine the mental pain, yet his instinctive reaction had been utterly selfish relief. He had never felt such shame. And she was quite adamant that he was not to approach her, leaving him with more guilt. He could not even tell her that he was sorry. What made these conflicting emotions even worse was that the relief persisted. For a long time, he sat, unmoving and wretched.

For the rest of the day, he behaved like an automaton. He kept active but he was largely unaware what he was doing. It was his subconscious in control. He had no appetite and ate nothing until the evening, when he recognized a strange feeling as hunger. He ate bread and cheese. He drank tea from time to time. Had he had any beer in the flat he might have drunk it, but from thirst rather than a desire for alcohol. Finally, exhausted, he went to bed, not expecting to sleep, but he did.

In the morning he got up and headed for the river out of habit. Beth arrived simultaneously. He nodded a good morning and turned, about to run.

"Gordon!" Beth made no move to start.

"What?"

"You look dreadful. Are you all right?"

"A bit tired," he said.

"I think it's time we sorted this out."

"Sorted what out?" She could have no idea about Sandra or the solicitors, surely.

"I'm not going to move until you've told me what this is about."

"I told you, I'm tired. I didn't sleep well," he lied.

"I'm not talking just about this morning. Ever since Gran died you've been acting strangely."

"I have no idea what you mean."

"I think you do. You seem to be avoiding me. You certainly don't talk to me, not even on the run."

"We should be concentrating on running. We do it for exercise after all."

"Is it something to do with Gran's death? Do you think I'm so delicate I can't hold a conversation?"

"No."

"I miss having a friend to talk to."

"Then talk to your boyfriend."

"My boyfriend?"

"Yes."

"I don't have a boyfriend, not in the sense I think you mean."

"Well, pardon me," said Gordon, irritable, annoyed at being lied to, "I know it's none of my business, but if he's enough of a friend to stay the night, I don't know what else to call him."

Beth stared at him, speechless for a moment. Then she obviously understood what he was alluding to. "Stayed overnight," she repeated, "You must mean John. On a motorbike?"

"Yes. And I happened to be in town another day and saw you together. You seem pretty close. He can hardly keep his hands off you."

Beth was still staring in disbelief. "John," she said, "is my brother."

"Your brother?"

"Yes. I'm sure I told you about him. He's a journalist."

Now he remembered. And now he felt very foolish. What was he thinking of? He tried to apologise, stammering, and blushing with embarrassment. The words would not come, and he waved his arms in a helpless gesture.

"It's only a silly mistake," she said. "It's not so bad to get upset about."

But for Gordon this was the culmination of emotional shocks which had started with the solicitor's letter. To his utter dismay, the realization of his clumsy and unjustified behaviour towards Beth, Beth who offered him friendship when he most needed it, overwhelmed him. He began to cry. He covered his face with his hands and slumped to the grass. Beth, concerned at his distress, sat down beside him and put her arms round him without speaking.

After a while he pulled away from her and wiped his face on the sleeve of his tracksuit. "Sorry," he said.

"It's not that serious," Beth insisted. "You've been a good friend to me. There's obviously something wrong other than a simple misunderstanding."

Gordon could not look her in the eyes. He drew up his knees and hugged them, staring at the water in the stream. "I'm not a very nice person," he said at last. "I don't think you would want to know me any better."

Beth looked at him curiously. He still looked away from her.

"You know the expression 'speak as you find'?" she said. " Well, you've always been kind as long as I've known you. Not long, I admit, but I can't see you as a secret murderer or something. Whatever it is, it's clearly upset you, and you don't have to tell me. You might feel better if you do though. I value your friendship." She slipped a hand under his arm, leaned over and, for the second time, kissed him on the cheek. Still without looking at her, Gordon began to tell her about Sandra. Once he began, the words poured out in a steady flood, like someone emptying the contents of a storage tank which had been blocked. He poured it out without looking at Beth. It was not until he spoke of the miscarriage that he paused, remembering who he was talking to. Then he stopped as he also realizes he was purging himself in yet another way, ignoring any discomfort or pain he might be causing Beth. Beth had said nothing, but she listened until he paused. Then he swore violently, disgusted at himself. "I'm so sorry," he said. "I have no right to burden you with all this. You won't want to pick up our friendship, not after all that. I'm so sorry."

He began struggling to his feet.

"Sit down," Beth commanded, "and listen to me."

He sat again, not looking at her. She was right to tell him how she felt, it was only fair.

"I have to admit I am surprised and quite shocked," she said. "Running away from this girl, Sandra, when she told you she was pregnant was unforgiveable. If you hadn't contacted her again, that would have been despicable. I'm not surprised she was angry. I can understand why she'd prefer to bring the child up on her own, rather than continue a relationship with a man who let her down. But you did at least resume contact."

"Too late," Gordon muttered.

"Yes, too late, perhaps, but you were ready to accept your responsibility in the end. That says something about your character."

"I can't forgive myself," Gordon said, "for feeling relieved because she's lost the baby. That's dreadful. What does that say about me?"

"Surely, it's not having to deal with debt, not the loss of the baby?"

Gordon though for a while. "I would never have wanted her to miscarry," he said, "That's true."

"I've known several women who have lost babies," said Beth. "It is a dreadful, traumatic business. Sandra will be in a very uncertain state. Don't think too badly of her. Give her time. She may come round in time. She may even want you back."

"No!" Gordon was vehement. "We weren't truly committed to one another like that, and it would be a disaster, even worse than this."

"You were obviously close, or it wouldn't have happened."

"We had fun together, that's all, that's all sex meant to us."

"Well, it's not for me to judge," said Beth, "but perhaps the relationship had run its course. Sandra clearly thinks so."

"And so do I. She is not someone I'd want to spend my life with, and she has made is plain I'm not the man for her."

"Then perhaps," said Beth, "it is as well the whole thing is over. Once you can find a hundred pounds to pay the solicitors, you can draw a line under it. I have to say I think there may be the tiniest trace of spite in the way she behaved."

That was a new thought.

"Beth," he said, looking at her this time, "I am very sorry to drag you into all this. It has ruined a friendship that was so valuable to me. Perhaps it's just as well we shall be losing our jobs in a few weeks. I'll find somewhere else for my run as from tomorrow and it shouldn't be too hard to keep out of your way."

"Don't be such a drama queen!" Beth's reply was unexpected. "Whatever you think about your own behaviour, it has nothing to do with our friendship. In fact, strangely enough, I feel privileged that you confided in me. Now, it's a bit late for a full run, but fifteen minutes each way will do us good." She stood up and brushed the grass from her clothes. Gordon did likewise and, as he straightened up, Beth kissed his tear-stained face and began to run.

For the rest of the day bits of the conversation echoed in Gordon's mind. He was confused and his emotions were in turmoil. He needed to escape, to be on his own. He got into his old car and drove almost at random until he turned up a country road that led to the top of the Sussex Downs. He wandered across the springy, sweet-smelling turf until he found somewhere to sit and overlook the Weald. The silence and the isolation soothed him. Together with Beth's kindness they reminded him that life might still have something pleasant, perhaps beautiful, to offer.

He had no compelling reason to return to Greenacres, but an idea had come to him and led him to drive into town. He went to the bank and spent an hour applying for a personal loan. It would be available, he was told, within a week. He would use the money to pay off Sandra's solicitor. He knew well the memory of this shameful interlude would not be wiped clean, but he would no longer be in direct contact. He had learned a great deal about himself, much of it unpleasant. He had also discovered a true friend in Beth. He thought about buying her some flowers but changed his mind. She could so easily misunderstand the gesture. He was still not totally confident of her continuing friendship.

He remained in town for the rest of the day and drove back in the early evening. He spent the evening listening to music.

Beth made no allusion to their conversation when they met the following morning. She merely smiled at him and led the way towards the bridge. She explained in a few words that she wanted to look at the cottage, which had already found a buyer.

There was nothing much to see except for an agent's sign in the front garden, announcing 'Under Offer'. There was nothing much to say, but Beth told Gordon the property had been snapped up immediately by a musician. He wanted a property where he could play music without disturbing neighbours and he had paid a surprisingly good price.

"I shall miss visiting the place," she said, "but I suppose I'd only feel sad every time I came back."

"I wonder if the new owner will tidy up the garden," Gordon said.

"Well, he'll need to sort out the inside first, I suppose," said Beth. "I can't imagine anyone wanting to leave it as it is."

"He would be well advised to install a water pump," Gordon remarked, unaware of the pun.

"I hope he's not short of money," Beth said. "It will be expensive to install electricity."

They did not stay long. Beth was looking sad as they headed back, and Gordon made no attempt to disturb her thoughts. He remembered that Beth had her own memories to cope with. She had been understanding the previous day, and he had not thought about her bereavement at the time. Yet again it struck him that he should try to be more sensitive.

Chapter ten

The lack of progress was frustrating, and all his colleagues treated The Bear with increasing caution. Inspector Carghill, who did not know him as well as many of his colleagues, was taken aback when simple questions met with rude responses. Sometimes the bad temper seemed unprovoked, sometimes it seemed a disproportionate response to a trivial enquiry or comment. When the Chief Inspector tried to contact one of the governors and was told the number was discontinued, he swore. "Mrs Beauchamp's list is out of date." He picked up the internal phone to speak to Irma Beauchamp. The line was dead, causing a further outpouring of colourful language. He left his desk and headed next door to the general office. He grabbed the doorknob in a huge paw and turned it with enough force to damage the mechanism. The door would not open. He tried again, rattling the doorknob so violently that Inspector Carghill heard him and the further barrage of blasphemies. The Bear pounded on the door. There was no response. Furious, he strode out through the front door and tried to peer in through the window. The window was a little high so he could not see much.

One of the teachers was passing, a man whose name The Bear had forgotten. He asked if there was a problem.

"Of course, there's a bloody problem," said The Bear. "The office door is locked."

"Maybe they overslept," suggested the teacher.

The Bear stared at him as though he was an imbecile before turning on his heel and heading back to his own desk. Inspector Carghill pretended to concentrate on the papers in front of him, The Bear picked up the internal phone again, cursing that he needed to look up another number, then dialled the Steward's House. That line was also dead. He slammed the receiver back in its cradle and left the office again in search of Sergeant Rawlings.

The Sergeant, familiar with his boss's moods, listened patiently, then told a constable to go to the Steward's House and ask Irma Beauchamp to come back to see the Chief Inspector. Then he made The Bear a mug of tea and listened some more, until the initial bad temper eased.

The constable returned looking apprehensive.

"Is she coming?" The Bear asked.

"There's no one there, sir," said the unfortunate constable.

"What do you mean, no one there?"

"They seem to have gone, sir. There's no sign of life inside. No one answered the door, and their car's gone."

"What the hell is going on?" asked The Bear, not expecting an answer. "Come on, Sergeant, we'll take a look for ourselves."

"If the place is locked," Rawlings pointed out, "there's not much we can do."

"We'll break in if we have to."

"Are you sure, sir?" It would be illegal, a matter of breaking and entering.

The Bear ignored the objection, however, and the three men marched off towards the Beauchamps' home.

The constable was right. The house appeared to be deserted.

"Break the glass," The Bear ordered as they stood outside the back door.

"Won't that be breaking and entering?" asked the constable.

"They could be lying dead in there," said The Bear. "Get on with it."

The constable picked up a convenient brick and broke the pane nearest the lock. He picked out the sharp, triangular shards, then reached inside. "There's no key in the lock," he said.

It was a sturdy, mortice lock. The Bear pushed the man aside and reached in himself, cutting his hand in the process. He swore loudly and did his best to wrap a none too clean handkerchief round his hand.

"Break the bloody door down," he ordered.

It was a solid, well-made door. There was no way it would open simply under the pressure of a shoulder barge. The constable lifted a heavily booted foot and aimed several blows near the lock. He damaged the paint but made little impression otherwise. The Bear was growing even more impatient. He looked around the area and spotted a rusty spade propped against a garden shed nearby, retrieved it and handed it to the younger man. Urged on by the big man, the constable used the tool as a battering ram in vain, then drove the blade into the crack between the door and frame and used it as a lever. Sergeant Rawlings looked on disapprovingly. What, he was thinking, would they say if the Beauchamps' campervan were to return at this point? But it did not return and, with a loud, splintering noise the door was broken. The lock fell to the floor with a heavy thump and the door swung open.

They entered through the kitchen, which was tidy but empty, like a holiday cottage awaiting new tenants. The Bear seized a clean tea towel to wrap round his hand and then led the way through the rest of the ground floor. The rooms all had the same, deserted look., There was nothing personal to be seen, no ornaments, no photographs. The telephone was in the sitting room. A glance revealed that the cord had been pulled out of the wall. There was no notepad nearby which might have yielded contact numbers. The entire house felt strangely sterile. The front door had both a mortice and a Yale lock and would have been harder still to break through.

Upstairs, the main bedroom yielded no information. The large wardrobe was empty, as were bedside cabinets. The double bed had been stripped. Another bedroom was also bare.

As they inspected the property, the constable said nothing, trying to avoid provoking The Bear unnecessarily. Rawlings observed in silence, drawing his own conclusions. The Bear was the only one of the three who spoke, but it was only to utter expletives as each room proved empty.

"Stay here," Rawlings ordered the constable. "I'll get the place secured. Don't let anyone in."

"So, they've scarpered," said The Bear. "Why? What do we know about them? Where will they be heading? And why?"

"You said all along there was something very fishy going on," said Rawlings, tactfully implying the boss deserved credit. "Do you think Inspector Carghill's enquiries are getting too hot for them? We don't actually know much about the Beauchamps, do we? We don't have much of an idea where they might go. The best we can do might be to track their campervan."

"Meanwhile," said The Bear, "we can't get at any of the school records. They're locked in the office. Are there any spare keys? We can't break down all the doors."

"Mrs Beauchamp kept the keys to every part of the school in her office." Rawlings was conscious of the irony. "I'll get a locksmith in."

While Rawlings got on with summoning a locksmith and a carpenter to repair the door of the Steward's House, The Bear phoned the Superintendent. Carghill could not have ignored the conversation, indeed he was deliberately included. What especially rankled with The Bear was that the Beauchamps must have planned their departure carefully in advance. This was not a sudden move, taken on the spur of the moment. He had been outplayed.

"We need more help, sir," he admitted. "Carghill here is convinced there is some kind of fraud involved. All this may have nothing to do with Mulcaster's death, of course, but it calls for a separate investigation."

The Superintendent said he would instigate a search for the campervan immediately before he drove to Greenacres. He wanted a meeting with The Bear, Carghill, Sir Lionel and Harold Black. As soon as the locksmith gained access to the school office, they could search for more information there. Carghill had already been exploring the accounts as far as possible, but they were extensive and involved authorizing access to several bank accounts. Greenacres was a complicated organisation, a business with a turnover of more than two million pounds. It employed forty-five people full-time. Income came from pupil fees, a sizeable contribution from the London bakery business, even rent from the farm and from those staff members in residence. A complete audit of the accounts would require a lot of expert manpower and take some time. The immediate need was to establish the exact nature of any malpractice. Carghill had already found discrepancies in the teachers' salaries.

Carghill was relieved at the prospect of a bigger scale investigation, although his part in it would be overshadowed by more senior officers. The Bear was dismayed and afraid that his murder investigation might be of less importance than an inquiry into fraud. There seemed to be a connection, but he could not see it.

The rest of the day was extremely busy. The meeting called by the Superintendent began with discussion with the members of the school staff and with Sir Lionel. It was aimed at discovering as much as was known of Frank and Irma Beauchamp. Even a phone call to Irma's previous employer revealed nothing much. Only one piece of information was of interest; the couple owned a property in Spain.

Halfway through the meeting there was a knock on the door and Sergeant Rawlings came in. He did not interrupt the discussion, but he brought with him an envelope which he placed in front of The Bear, before leaving as unobtrusively as he came in. The Bear opened it and read the note in the Sergeant's handwriting.

"A man called John Shepherd wanted to speak to you. Said he had information that could be important. He's a reporter. Told him you were busy, but I think you will want to speak to him asap."

The Bear folded the note and put it back in the envelope. He did not much like reporters. If Sergeant Rawlings thought the information might be useful, then he would fit him in once the meeting was over and the follow-up arrangements had been made. The name Shepherd was familiar, but he didn't know any local reporters of that name. There was so much to do, however, that The Bear forgot the envelope until the Super left and Sir Lionel limped to his car, extremely worried at the catastrophic turn of events adumbrated by the forthcoming, financial investigations. Fortunately, the Governors were individually protected by an indemnity insurance. Had they not been, and had they faced personal responsibility for the debts they might all have been contemplating financial ruin. As things stood, they would have to shoulder the blame for their joint failure to oversee the proper conduct of Greenacres School.

Rawlings had once again proven his remarkable ability as an organiser. He had asked Mrs Hastings, the school cook, to prepare a hot meal. Rawlings led his boss to the staff dining room and joined him and Cargill with a plate of lasagne and a bottle of beer. It was only then that The Bear remembered the note. He took it out of his pocket and waved it.

"Who's this chap?" he asked.

"A man called Shepherd, boss. He calls himself an investigative journalist."

"And what does he claim he has found out?"

"He says he has been working on a story about two young boys at Merryman School."

"What's that to do with Greenacres?"

"Mulcaster was Headmaster of Merryman."

The Bear grunted acknowledgement that there might be a connection, if slight.

"The two boys in question were badly bullied," Rawlings continued. "The parents complained to Mulcaster but he refused to interfere. Apparently, he said they had to learn to stand up for themselves."

"A bit harsh!"

"The two boys were not related, and the parents had nothing to do with one another, but each set of parents took their son out of the school."

The Bear was finding it difficult to sustain interest. It had been a demanding day. "Get to the point," he said, "What has all this to do with Greenacres?"

"Both boys committed suicide at different times, soon after leaving Merryman. They both left notes to say bullying had ruined their lives. That's what Shepherd is investigating."

"I still don't see."

"One father swore he would get even with Mulcaster."

"Ah! I see. But Merryman School is, what, fifty miles from here."

"The father in question, a man called Curtis, is the brother-in-law of Aled Williams."

All at once The Bear was wide awake. "The same Williams who teaches here?"

Rawlings nodded. "The same. The boy, Ben Curtis, was William's nephew."

The Bear thought for a few minutes. "It seems a little remote, but I don't like coincidences," he said. "Can we get this Shepherd in tomorrow?"

"No problem," said Rawlings. "Another coincidence."

The big man looked enquiringly. "John Shepherd is the brother of Beth Shepherd."

"The Domestic Science teacher?"

"Yes. He's staying with her tonight."

As he made his weary way home a little later, The Bear was thinking the latest lead was a weak one, but it was at least a lead and would keep him busy for a while.

The following day marked a major change in the investigation. Rawlings was kept busy reorganising the space. It was as well that this was not term time, because the Superintendent's conversations with New Scotland Yard sparked a serious response. Fraud, The Bear reflected sourly, was viewed as more demanding of resources than homicide. Rawlings was asked to prepare at least three rooms for specialist officers. The first of them arrived at lunchtime and wasted no time before Carghill was interrogated about what he knew so far.

At least it meant he would no longer be working in the same office as The Bear. As soon as Rawlings had explained what the visiting team required, The Bear was happy to leave him in charge while he sent for John Shepherd.

"You say there's a connection between this man Williams and Mulcaster?"

"Not a direct connection."

"Then what are you saying?"

"Aled Williams was uncle to a pupil at Merryman School. The boy was withdrawn after complaints of bullying, but he then killed himself. He left a note saying the bullying had ruined his life. His father, Williams' brother-in-law, made threats against Mulcaster. I have been investigating Mulcaster and his policy, or lack of policy towards bullying. When I heard that he had been killed in suspicious circumstances, shortly after being made Head here, at Greenacres, I wondered if his past might have caught up with him, but it was only when I discovered the link between Williams and Merryman, that I really smelled a rat."

"Why didn't you tell us about this earlier?"

"I didn't know Williams worked here until my sister mentioned him casually two days ago."

"Why did your sister think Williams was hiding something?"

"She didn't. I told you, it was a casual remark. I had interviewed his sister and her husband, and they had mentioned their son's uncle. The name was unusual, Aled is not exactly common, very Welsh."

"Was Williams also threatening revenge?"

"Well, no, not according to his sister. When I explained I was investigating the two suicides, Mrs Curtis said she hoped the truth would come out so that the bullying would stop, but also that it would start a more general debate about bullying as a problem. She told me that was how her brother thought."

"But you believe he wanted violence?"

"I'm not saying that."

"Then what are you saying?"

"Only that there is a connection between Williams and Mulcaster that you should know about, and it predates Mulcaster's arrival at Greenacres."

"I see."

The Bear sat in the empty office when Shepherd had gone and tried to work out the significance or lack of significance of the reporter's information. Williams might have had a motive for interfering with Mulcaster's car, but, if he had wanted the man to be unmasked, killing him was an unlikely way to achieve it. He swung the chair round and stared out of the window at the green foliage opposite. He had spoken to Williams only a matter of hours ago. The man was quiet, relaxed, polite. Unless this was a case of still waters running extraordinarily deep, he was the most unlikely man to resort to violence. His attitude towards Wilder suggested he was a man of compassion rather than a man of violence. Yet the new information could not be completely ignored.

There were too many possible suspects in this case. Wilder apart, no one seemed to have a strong enough motive. Now the Fraud Squad was moving in, there was no knowing what particularly evil-looking creatures might crawl out from under stones. He would need to stay closely informed as that part of the enquiry continued.

He made his way to the staff dining room where the head cook made him tea and gave him a slice of cake. The ground floor of the main building, the rooms of which were originally used as a school, now had in effect become a fair-sized police station. There was plenty of room for the new personnel, but The Bear was pleased that he had been in position first. It meant he could keep possession of the headmaster's office, and, Inspector Carghill would vacate his desk, since he would be included in the fraud investigation. The Bear had nothing against Carghill, but he was pleased to have the office to himself once more.

One thing left him uneasy; the senior investigating officer in the Fraud Squad held the same rank, Chief Inspector. The two enquiries would proceed in parallel, but should there be a dispute between The Bear and his opposite number, DCI Manley, it would require the intervention of a higher-ranking officer, either the Superintendent The Bear knew, or an officer in London. The only hope was that the two enquiries could proceed comfortably together yet independently.

The difficulty, which The Bear foresaw might arise when the Beauchamps were found. As things stood it would be difficult to charge them with any crime. DCI Manley and his team could find something quickly.

He need not have worried. He had been back at his desk only an hour when Manley came to see him.

"This looks like being an interesting can of worms," he said. "Carghill has picked up the first abnormality. Beauchamp issued individual contracts to each member of staff and told them not to share information."

"That did sound unusual," The Bear agreed.

"But not illegal," said Manley. "Carghill collected contracts from half a dozen of the teachers and compared them, line by line, with the versions kept on file and held by

Beauchamp. On average the teachers' contracts give a net figure one percent below those showns on file."

"Is that significant?"

"Oh yes. The average salary is about fifteen thousand. One percent is one hundred and fifty. There are nearly fifty employees, giving a total skim-off of £7,500."

"Each year?"

"Yes, meaning, just from that source, Beauchamp has embezzled about £30,000 in four years."

"You say 'just from that source'" said The Bear. "There's more?"

"Much more, but it will take time to track it down. The salary scam is chickenfeed. A big area is the way all the insurances were organized. The money has ended up mostly in secret accounts in the Channel Islands in specially created companies. We are expecting this to run into at least two million pounds. We shan't be able to track that down for some time yet, but the salaries business is already pretty clear fraud, and we can charge Beauchamp with false accounting as soon as he's found."

"What about his wife?"

"No evidence yet, but she must have known all about it. We'll probably be able to tie her in at some point."

"So," said The Bear, "the sooner we find them, the better."

"Yes, absolutely."

"This doesn't seem to help me much in finding the person who caused the death of Mulcaster."

"It seems not. Sorry about that."

"Keep me informed. I'll redouble our effort to trace the Beauchamps. I take it that is their right name? What do you think?"

"Worth some serious digging, I'd say. We can leave that to you, I imagine?"

It was a far more amicable arrangement than The Bear had anticipated.

The more he thought about it, the more certain he became that Beauchamp was an assumed name. His team, whose interest had begun to flag, responded to his instruction to concentrate on investigating the Beauchamps. The school governors squirmed as they were obliged to think again about the time when the new

Secretary and then the new Bursar had been appointed. Previous employers were also interviewed. The appointments had been approved in both cases with the flimsiest reference. Only one referee in each case had been contacted by telephone. Irma Beauchamp had been properly employed in the insurance company, but her husband's appointment had been totally informal. No one asked about his personal, financial history.

A very interesting search through the records failed to find a marriage certificate in which a Frank Beauchamp had married anyone. Guessing at Frank Beauchamp's age suggested a hunt through birth records might help. They found no one.

It was chance that led to their discovery. A possible route they might have taken was to the ferry port of Dover. It was within easy driving distance, and it was believed the Beauchamps owned a holiday home in Spain. The port authorities were alerted, but there was no sign of the campervan. A police patrol car, driving on a B road some twenty miles from the port, was passing a small garage when the driver glimpsed a van parked at the rear. Ordinarily he would have driven on, but he had seen an alert for a Volkswagen van. He pulled in. It was the van in question. The driver had been heading for Dover one morning when he had suffered a serious breakdown – the rear axle had broken. The driver and his wife, the garage owner explained, were staying at a cottage in the village which advertised bed and breakfast. Three hours later, they were back at Greenacres.

DCI Manley charged Beauchamp with false accounting. His wife was told to stay at Greenacres or face charges of perverting the course of justice or of wating police time. The fraud investigation now took precedence, Photographs and fingerprint records revealed the man's name was Frank Beresford and he had a record of petty offences. There were no records for his wife, but they had been married for six years. When Frank was released from a six-month prison sentence, they had simply assumed the name of Beauchamp.

None of this suggested to the Bear it would lead directly or indirectly to the person who had interfered with Mulcaster's car. He called Williams back after Shepherd's information. His own enthusiasm was also flagging, like that of his team, and he had only the faintest hope that the interview would lead anywhere.

"Chief Inspector," said Williams, taking his place in the chair opposite the tired, scowling policeman. "What can I do for you?"

"Tell me about your nephew," The Bear said bluntly.

A look of real surprise crossed Williams' face. "My nephew?" he repeated.

"Your late nephew. Ben was his name, I believe."

Williams' expression changed as though The Bear had stabbed him. "Why are you asking me about Ben?" he asked.

"I understand the boy took his own life," said The Bear. He spoke in a neutral tone. "Shortly after leaving Merryman School."

Williams was staring at him resentfully. "That is a matter of record," he said, "but why do you feel the need to bring it up?"

"Were you close to your nephew?"

"Yes."

"And I presume you were aware that he blamed the school, said he was bullied by pupils and teachers alike?"

"Yes."

"So, what was your reaction when you learned Mulcaster was to take over here as headmaster?"

"I was appalled, upset, angry. What do you expect?"

"Angry enough to tamper with his car?"

"What?" The reaction was exactly what The Bear had hoped to provoke. Williams was no longer the quietly confident, controlled person he appeared to be, but he was well and truly rattled. The Bear knew that provoking a violent, emotional response like this left his victim vulnerable. In such a state he would blurt out all kinds of things, reveal hidden truths, often incriminate himself.

Williams was staring at the big man without speaking until he regained control of his feelings. The angry flush faded and The Bear saw outrage and anger change slowly into an expression he seldom saw. It was contempt.

"Maybe, Chief Inspector," he said slowly and distinctly, "it's time you gave up your job. You obviously judge everyone by your own standards. I thought policemen believed in the rule of law, that they looked for evidence and facts, not twisted and prejudiced assumptions. Let me say just once, I had nothing to do with the death of the repugnant Mulcaster. Find some evidence before you accuse any other innocent bystander."

At that he stood up and left the room.

The Bear stared at the closed door. Williams' reaction had been much as he had expected and seemed quite genuine. He did not feel especially sorry to have upset the teacher. Poking a stick into a wasps' nest would always result in painful consequences; he himself wore his professional indifference like personal armour.

Nevertheless, the current lines of enquiry had led nowhere, except to reveal various kinds of fraud. Ironically, it would be DCI Manley and his team who would get the credit for solving that. He needed to take a step back and try another angle – but what? He left his office and wandered round the building as far as the car park where the damage to Mulcaster's car had taken place.

Beth Shepherd and her brother were looking at the place where the car had been left. John Shepherd nodded.

"How come the brake liquid didn't leave a stain?" he asked.

"Whoever did it must have put a dish underneath," said The Bear.

"What, and carried it away somewhere? Wouldn't that be taking a big chance?"

"Yes, if he took it very far."

"Why not pour it down the drain?"

"The nearest drain is inside the courtyard. We'd have found traces, anyway.y"

He left them standing there. He was not in the mood to talk. He had thought about this oil business many times before.

He sat for a while and watched the ducks. He was tired. He could not think of a way forward.

Chapter eleven

As he jogged down to the river, Gordon saw that Beth had brought her brother. He was not dressed for running but wore an old pair of trousers and a sweater.

"Hallo," he said, holding out his hand.

"You're not running like that, are you?"

"Not a chance. You're honoured I got up early enough to meet you."

Gordon laughed. "You don't know what you're missing," he said.

"I do. My bed."

They laughed. Beth was evidently pleased the two men got on well.

"I'm John," said Beth's brother, "and I know you're Gordon. I should thank you."

"Thank me? What for?"

"Being a good friend to my little sister when I wasn't here."

"She's been a good fried to me, too." Gordon smiled at Beth. There was no need to explain."

"I wanted to tell you we have a date for Gran's funeral. Do you still want to come?" Beth was looking at him.

"Of course."

"You can go back to bed, if you like," said Beth to her brother.

"I don't think I will," John said. "That floor is pretty hard. Make sure you get a flat with a spare bedroom next time."

"I'm interviewing for a new job next Wednesday," Bed told Gordon. "It's a step up, lecturer in a university department."

"Wow!"

"Come on," Beth said, turning onto the footpath. "We're getting cold."

He was going to miss her, Gordon thought, as they ran in single file as far as the trees. She had become an important friend. She would not be more than a friend, though. She was an attractive girl, good-looking, athletic, with a sense of fun. She had proved herself as a listener and he was sure she would never betray his confidences. He had also seen her at her most vulnerable. But he had learned a lesson from his affair with Sandra. He would never enter into a relationship with the same degree of irresponsibility, and certainly not with Beth. He was pleased for her, assuming she got the job. It made him think again about his own future post Greenacres.

By mutual consent they ran more energetically, not speaking much. They were breathless when they got back. Gordon headed for the entrance hall after breakfast. The arrival of the second contingent of policemen and their occupation of three more classrooms meant the notice boards had expanded. The new Detective Chief Inspector had taken over a small room as his personal office.

The posting of a uniformed constable outside the Steward's House had aroused curiosity, but the entire property was taped off. Harold Black and his wife, who lived next door, had a grandstand view, and Harold was one of the first to be informed officially of the search for the missing couple. The Governors convened and DCI Manley explained the reasons for the search. Harold recognised the criminality as a terrible betrayal of trust, not only by the Beauchamps, but also by the Governors themselves. Their consternation and near panic were, he realised, more to do with the personal consequences for themselves than the effect this would have on the school. For him, Harold Black, Greenacres School had become his life. It was about to be destroyed. He did not especially care that he would probably never find another post like his present one, but the closure of the school felt like the death of a loved one.

Not so his wife: the revelation of the Beauchamps' fraud and the Governors' negligence provided Thelma with fuel to intensify the acrimony that had smouldered for so long in her soul. She was permanently disappointed by her husband, whom she saw as a weak shadow of a man, a failure lacking in drive or ambition. If only he had seized his chances, argued his way into a more forceful role, he could have taken charge years ago, while the old headmaster, clearly ineffectual and uninterested, should have been driven out. But Harold was far too weak. and he had not even glimpsed where the slackness of the Governors was leading. She had warned him tirelessly to show more initiative, to try to summon up a sense of purpose which, deep down, she knew was never there.

She was standing at her kitchen window when a police car drew up outside the Steward's House. She took off her apron and stepped outside in time to see the constable winding up the tape. From the back seat of the car a policeman emerged, followed by Irma Beauchamp. Where was Frank? Was he under arrest? Why had Irma been brought back here? If they were responsible for the death of Mulcaster, surely, they should both be in a secure prison cell. The constable unloaded two large boxes, presumably Irma's clothes, maybe bedding. Thelma's curiosity burned fiercely. She returned inside, tidied her hair hastily, locked the door carefully, and set off at a brisk walk for the school building, taking a good look at her neighbours' property on the way.

She was hunting for her husband. She did not have to look far. He was in the general office, at the desk normally occupied by Irma Beauchamp, and he was on the phone. He looked even more harassed than usual.

"Harold," Thelma enquired loudly, "what's going on?"

Her husband pointed at the telephone in his hand and did not reply. The caller was clearly demanding his full attention, though Harold appeared unable to get a word in. Finally, he announced, "I am very sorry, but this is beyond our control, but we shall be in touch shortly," then he put the phone down quickly. It rang again almost at once.

"Harold!" Thelma demanded his attention.

"I'm very busy, Thelma," he said as the bell continued to demand his attention. "Word has got out that the school secretary is not answering the phone. Someone has to deal with the parents and the press."

"The press! This isn't your job," she told him. "You should find someone else."

"Thelma," he spoke more loudly than usual, competing with the telephone bell, "This is an emergency. The DCI is arranging for someone else to..." At this point the door swung open, nearly knocking an angry Thelma off her feet, and a young policewoman came in. She walked straight over to Harold, nodded a silent greeting, and picked up the phone. In the sudden calm she spoke into the receiver, "Greenacres School. Please ring off unless this is an emergency." Thelma and Harold stared at the young woman as the caller tried to continue the conversation. "I'm sorry," the policewoman repeated, "we are unable to deal with calls at the moment." She put the phone down. It rang again immediately. She let it ring a few times as Harold and Thelma made their escape. "We are unable to accept any calls at the moment," the young woman was saying, as the couple emerged into the entrance hall.

"What is going on?" Thelma repeated. "Irma Beauchamp has just returned under police guard without her husband. She is back in their house. That's not right. We can't be expected to be living next door to a murderer."

"Murderer? Who said she was a murderer?"

"Why else would they run away? And why aren't they under arrest? They should be in prison."

"Thelma," her husband said in his customary, patiently resigned tone. We don't know what's going on, but I expect Frank Beauchamp has been up to some nasty tricks, fiddling the accounts. That' what this new lot of police are up to. It looks as though he made a bolt for it but didn't get far."

"You must know what's going on, you're spending all your time here. That awful Inspector Whatever his name is, the one who took over your office, he must tell you what's happening. You're entitled to know. And why has it taken so long to send that chit of a girl to answer the phone?"

Harold, his head already ringing from the telephone bell, the angry and aggressive callers demanding answers, and now his wife's 'hectoring tones, held up a weary hand. "It's all over," he said. "The school is finished, and my career with it."

"What are you talking about?"

"Thelma," he said, suddenly looking curiously relaxed, "Greenacres School is finished, ruined. From now on it's the police who are in charge. They don't need or want my help. They are dealing with the press. They will demand the Governors take responsibility for dealing with the parents. Bankers and solicitors will sort everything else. There will be no more pupils."

Thelma stared at him, open-mouthed.

"But you are the acting headmaster!" she said.

"Of a non-existing school; And do you know? I'm relieved. All at once I'm free."

"What about me? If your job here is over, where are we going to live? Have you got another job in mind?"

"No," said Harold, and he smiled, an unusual and unexpected change of expression which she failed to understand. For a moment she suspected the strain of the past week or so might have unhinged him. She was frightened. But Harold changed as she stood in the familiar hall that smelled of stale food and floor polish. He squared his shoulders and, astonishingly, laughed lightly.

"I think I might do a bit of traveling," he said. "I've got an endowment policy I can cash in."

"Travel? Won't we need to buy a house?"

"Thelma," he said firmly, looking her in the eyes, "you can do what you want. We'll come to an agreement about money, but when I said travel, I meant on my own."

"Don't be ridiculous!"

"I should have done it years ago. Even you have to agree it has not been a very successful marriage."

"You were never ambitious enough. I tried to get you to improve yourself."

"Yes, you certainly nagged me enough, but never once have you thought about what I wanted, only what I should do to get you what you want."

"I thought you might have achieved something if you really tried."

"I've never been interested much in status. That's all you ever wanted."

Thelma looked at her husband as though seeing him for the first time. They had met when he was in his twenties. Now, thirty years had passed, and she realised she had seldom seen him smile or heard him laugh. His entire life had been bound up with this school, yet he had never been entirely happy, just burdened with responsibility. He had been given a role as disciplinarian, a role he disliked, since his relationship with the boys was perforce based on underlying fear, not on a respect which stemmed from admiration. Yet, despite his lack of ambition, until this moment Greenacres had been his entire life. Smashing the institution into fragments would, she thought, have been like destroying his world. Instead, he saw it as freedom. His ridiculous dream of retiring to wander who knew where on his own could probably be ended, but it might prove very hard to find another post at his age. For once she could find nothing else to say. She uttered an angry expression of impatience and walked out of the hall.

Harold turned on his heel, intending to leave by the front door to seek the quiet of the lawn. Aled Williams was standing in front of him, an embarrassed look on his face.

"Ah, Aled," Harold said without a sign of embarrassment himself, "how much of that did you hear?"

"Enough," said Williams. "I'm sorry."

"Don't be," said Harold. "It's a relief to say these things. I really do feel free all at once."

"You look as though you need someone to talk to."

"Maybe." Harrold raised his eyebrows to indicate uncertainty. "That's one of the many disadvantages of being deputy head. You don't make many friends."

"Well," said Williams, "I imagine you won't be too keen to go home at the moment."

Harold laughed, something Williams had never witnessed before. He was surprised in the circumstances.

"Fancy a cup of tea?" he suggested. "My flat's on the first floor."

Harold followed him out of the hall and up to the flat. Inside, he sat in a comfortable chair as Williams filled a kettle and talked through the open doorway. Harold was looking round the sitting room. Two of the walls were lined with books. Like everything else in the room, they were neatly arranged. There was also a small bookcase which doubled as a coffee table. There was a tray on the table to protect it. On one wall there was an array of framed photographs of a wide range of subject-matter, a dozen pictures of individuals, three family groups, two or three individuals were in military uniform, several quite spectacular pictures of birds. Harold noticed two full shelves of books were on ornithological topics. There was a modest but probably expensive record player and a number of long-play records, but he could not see the labels. The furniture was simple and comfortable. A good-sized desk against another wall was furnished with a typewriter and an Anglepoise lamp. Harold mentally contrasted it with his own home. Thelma had failed to turn a selection of furniture into any more than that. There were no photographs in display there, just dull reproductions of dull paintings, none of which had any personal significance.

Williams came in with the tea. "I didn't ask if you'd prefer something stronger," he said. "I don't drink, so I couldn't offer you anything. Welsh Primitive Methodism is the cause."

"You realise," said Harold, "I know next to nothing about you. You'd think I'd know my colleagues as part of my job."

"You've had your hands full doing the headmaster's job," Williams observed. "The old man did next to nothing."

"I suppose you're right."

" As schools go," Williams observed, settling back in his chair, "Greenacres is pretty poor, but that's not your fault."

The judgement held no malice, but Harold was shocked by the bald statement. His normal reaction would have been to refute it, defend the school, speak of the long tradition, the original vision of its founder. Today, however, he was ready to concede he had been publicly fighting a losing battle for years. Remarks he had heard in the past from disillusioned staff members and parents alike, which he had argued against out of a felt need to show loyalty, today felt true. The institution which he had always pretended to himself was struggling against unfair changes in the parents' attitude over the years had collapsed in ruins. He was depressed by the collapse, but also relieved that he had acknowledged the truth. He was glad the fight was over, just like his miserable marriage. He had no need to pretend any longer.

"I'll be honest," he said, nursing the delicate cup in his hands, "standards have fallen steadily. The quality of the teaching staff has fallen to match. You are one of the few teachers who have done a good job. I don't know why you've stayed so long."

"I like the boys," Williams replied. "A lot of them don't have much of a home life. Most of them are perhaps of only average ability. They'll end up in boring jobs. A lot of them lack ambition. That doesn't mean they are in any way worthless, and I want to give them a taste of excellence. I try to share some of the satisfaction I get myself from books, poetry, traditional things like the English countryside."

"You could easily have moved on to a better school," said Harold. "You might have found it more rewarding, better pupils and more supportive parents."

Williams put down his cup, clasped his hands behind his head and gazed at the pictures on the wall.

"I suppose I could have," he admitted, "but I'm also quite lazy. I get on well with the boys, so the work itself isn't over-demanding. I have perfectly comfortable quarters, and moving would be a bore. Then, we live in glorious countryside. The holidays are usually uncluttered and I'm paid well enough to do with them what I want. I've visited twenty-five countries on bird-watching trips.!

"But no wife." Harold was looking for a flaw.

"No, no wife. You'll forgive me if I don't give you an account of my love life, I hope. Maybe I'm lucky in that respects. I've seen a few bad marriages in my time."

They fell silent. Williams poured more tea. Harold could not remember a time when he had felt so relaxed in the company of a colleague. He was thinking how he seemed to have missed something. After a while he stirred himself.

"What are your immediate plans?" Williams asked.

"I'll have to stick around for a while. Now the cat's out of the bag, and the press have got wind of a scandal, I suppose I'll be a bit of a go-between between the police and them."

"Sir Lionel is already taking it hard."

"I didn't realise you were in his confidence."

"We have an understanding," Williams explained. "I try to keep a fatherly eye on Stephen Wilder for him. You know he's Sir Lionel's godson, I take it?"

"Yes," Harold admitted. "He should never have been appointed in the first place. The number of problems he has caused!"

"You're right," Williams agreed, "but the poor chap is ill, and with good cause."

"Then he should be receiving treatment, this is a completely inappropriate place for him."

"These things are not straightforward. I've seen a good few men whose lives have been ruined because of their war experiences."

"You realise Wilder is the prime suspect for tampering with the brakes on Mulcaster's car?"

"He didn't do it."

"You sound definite."

"I am. Stephen Wilder may be an alcoholic, a misfit, someone who speaks his mind with no care for others, he may even be incompetent as a teacher, but he is not malicious. He is to be pitied. I don't think I've ever known a man more deserving of pity."

Harold was taken aback by the strength of feeling. He moved towards the door.

"What about you?" Williams asked, walking with him to the door. "You're going to find it uncomfortable at home."

"I'll move out. I'll use the headmaster's flat for the moment."

As he looked for the housekeeper, to tell her to make up a bed for him, Harold was smiling. It was ironic, he was thinking, that he would now occupy the headmaster's flat, which Thelma had coveted for so long. She saw it as a sign of status, but he was moving in out of necessity, while the institution that had been Greenacres School, was reduced to nothing.

Chapter twelve

The fatal crash which had triggered so much had aroused little interest in the local press. A one-inch column mentioned the unfortunate coincidence of the deaths of two headmasters in quick succession. It was the outrage expressed by several parents at the postponement of the term dates which provoked some interest. The involvement of the police aroused more interest and Irma Beauchamp had at first fielded a few, telephone queries. A second postponement and a suggestion that the future was uncertain had resulted in a growing volume of calls demanding clearer information. Pupil withdrawals reached the point where the school looked set to close its doors. The Governors met daily, but they had little room to manoeuvre all the time the police investigation, led by DCI Blundell, continued. Local journalists sensed a story was about to break, but they were concerned principally with the social and educational consequences of the closure of the school. It had been part of the educational landscape for over eighty years.

The Governors were badly shaken and unaccustomed to dealing with a crisis on such a scale. The opening of a separate enquiry into the possible maladministration and fraud came as an even worse shock. Unaccustomed to such problems, they met, listened to briefings by DCIs Manley and Blundell and discussed the situation endlessly. They contacted the Charity Commissioners and were depressed further as they were told of further action to follow. At least this had happened during the school holidays. If the Governors had followed the advice off their legal advisers and of the police, matters might have continued to be uncomfortable and tense until the procedures reached their conclusion. Unfortunately, one or two of the Governors were indiscreet, and too ready to talk to journalists. This opened the way for more questions, many of them addressed directly to the police teams. The Bear did not take kindly to such interference and was distracted from his main work to try to hunt down the source of the leaks. He asked the WPC he told to respond to phone calls to take note of each caller, many of whom were anxious or angry parents. Calls from members of the press got no reply except notification of press conferences which the two DCIs called and planned together.

They gave little away. As a consequence of investigating the death of Mulcaster, they announced, certain irregularities had come to light. The investigations concerned financial irregularities and the school would be unable to reopen for the foreseeable future. The vague nature of this announcement led to questions about the future viability of the school, the employment prospects for the staff, questions which grew rapidly more raucous as some of the parents joined in. It was all difficult to deal with.

Legally, the Governors were responsible, but the police teams exerted a powerful control. Legal advisers joined in the fun, both those retained ordinarily and those appointed by the Charity Commissioners. The London Bakery which had provided financial support to the school for eighty years was busy wriggling out of the legal ties. The banks, their accounts already looked at by the Fraud Squad, were no longer cooperative.

Within a few days of the brief flight by the Beauchamps, (the name continued in use), the Governors felt it necessary to follow the advice of the police by no longer using members of the school staff to deal with official enquiries or answer any questions from the public. A WPC answered the telephone. Sir Lionel was busy helping the police. As days passed, even Harold Black was seldom consulted. The rest of the staff were asked to remain on the campus for two weeks after the Beauchamps had been recaptured. At the end of that time, they were asked to give addresses and phone numbers in the UK where they could be reached at any time, but many remained in the accommodation they occupied at the school. Others set off on an increasingly anxious quest for another job. At the end of two weeks, The Bear and his team packed up equipment and boxes of papers and returned to their familiar offices in town. The Beauchamps, after being exhaustively and repeatedly interviewed by the Fraud team, were remanded in custody. Their interrogations continued frequently as the DCI continued to uncover details.

The funeral of Beth's grandmother took place in the second week. There were only a few mourners, including Gordon. Afterwards there was a small reception in a local hotel. The sale of the cottage was agreed, and the buyer was eager to move in. He had paid well and Beth's share, she said, would enable her to buy a property for herself. She was quite excited at the prospect of her new post, which would be more challenging than her work at Greenacres. She and Gordon had continued their daily run, and Gordon knew he would miss her.

John, her brother, was still researching the bullying story. Reporting his discovery of the link between Aled Williams and the deaths of former Merryman pupils had led nowhere in the end. The Bear had failed to uncover a close connection between Williams and the sabotage of Mulcaster's vehicle.

It began to look as if the person responsible for Mulcaster's death would never be satisfactorily identified. The Bear had renewed his questioning of two suspects, Stephen Wilder, who was the far more likely culprit, and Clifford Jackson. Jackson was an arrogant nan, but he had the skill and opportunity to cut the brake pipes. The workshop, from which he could collect tinsnips and, equally importantly, a tray to collect the drained oil, was close by Mulcaster's parking space. The tray was important. Without it the grass would be clearly stained. Disposing of the brake fluid was also important. Anyone carrying such a tray would be conspicuous as it would have to be carried horizontally until it could be emptied. Where better to do that than in the workshop itself? But Jackson had an alibi. His friend Jessie had been interviewed and she confirmed his story.

Stephen Wilder undoubtedly had the stronger motive, but was he physically capable? Unless new evidence came to light, the original enquiry could get no further. Everyone, including The Bear, was left frustrated. The staff, very shortly to lose both their jobs and their homes, remained angry as well as anxious. The Governors tried to soften the blow by allowing a few to remain in the school accommodation until January. The anger was directed in roughly equal proportions against the Governors, the Beauchamps and the police.

Beth had never been particularly involved socially with the male staff. The daily run with Gordon had been an unusual friendship. She would not greatly miss Greenacres which would always be associated in her mind with the death of her grandmother. Her association with Gordon was relatively casual, despite the few intense moments they had shared. Neither of them was romantically interested. So, Beth was preoccupied with the new post in a red brick university I the northwest, while Gordon had found a temporary job in a busy hotel in the south-west. It offered a low wage, long hours and somewhere to sleep and eat. The hotel offered a range of outdoor and sporting activities to the guests. Gordon would help with some of those. He would also serve in the restaurant and undertake whatever work fell his way. It would give him breathing space, while he considered what he might do with his life.

He still hankered after a full-time job as a professional sportsman, but he could see no way of doing that. Meanwhile, with time on his hands, he sought out the master in charge of PE and got him to allow access to the school gymnasium. It was well equipped. The teacher, Granger, was reluctant at first, concerned about liability and insurance, but Gordon wrote him a signed note waiving such claims. Granger then proved helpful, setting out a program for Gordon to follow. Thus, every morning, on returning from the run, Gordon undertook a full hour of exercise, designed to improve all aspects of his physical fitness.

He had never been a full member of the community in the short time he spent at Greenacres. He had not been there when the place was alive with scores of boys, bustling with the energy of youth. With no prospect of the school opening again, even Gordon sensed the atmosphere of despair that accompanied the disintegration. The common purpose of the staff was to teach pupils. Without that shared purpose the individuals had much less in common. They were heading off in every direction.

Gordon experienced an instinctive need to counter this sense of decay so, unasked and without seeking approval, he took the tractor from its shed and cut the grass. One or two residents paused to watch, then shrugged and went on their way. Harold Black stepped out of the main door to meet Sir Lionel and tackle the work in the office. Both men stopped, then turned towards the tractor. Harold held up a hand. Gordon stopped the tractor near the two men.

"Good morning," he said.

"Good morning," Harold replied. "Did someone ask you to cut the grass?"

"No. It was getting very untidy, so I thought it might be a good idea."

"Excellent!" Sir Lionel observed. "We shouldn't let the place get overgrown. It helps cheer everyone up. Well done, young man."

"Thank you," said Gordon, climbing back into the driving seat."Oh, I shan't be able to do this again unless someone can order some petrol. Without the Bursar, I don't know who to ask."

"Where did this come from?" asked Harold.

"There are several jerry-cans in the groundsman's shed."

"Right, If you can bring them up to the car park, I arrange for them to be refilled."

"And thank you again," Sir Lionel added.

September slipped into October. After a week of misty weather, one morning dawned bright and clear. It was chilly as the two runners set off along the familiar path. The trees, Gordon noted, were changing colour and beginning to shed their leaves. Autumn was arriving to add to the melancholy surrounding Greenacres. Beth admitted she felt sad, even though she was not especially attached to the school.

"I suppose," she said, "it's because the school has existed over seventy years. All that history, all those pupils, even all those staff, consigned to history."

"I suppose so," said Gordon. " But, from all accounts, it wasn't a very good school."

"Maybe not, but you can't write it off just like that. I have never mixed much with the staff – a lot of them are sexist, chauvinists – but there are several good ones. There are even one or two really good teachers."

"Oh?" Gordon was interested to hear Beth's judgements.

"Aled Williams is probably the best teacher. He seems to get the boys interested in books. Ray Carpenter is also good with the boys."

"Harold Black?"

Beth did not reply at first. Then, "He had the worst job of all," she said. "As deputy Head, he was expected to be the hatchet man. It must be very wearing to begin every day with a queue of miscreant teenagers. They can be very difficult, hostile, aggressive, uncooperative. Harold Black had them all. Then he had Thelma to cope with at home."

"I take it you feel sorry for him."

"Yes, I do. But it seems he and Thelma have split. And he won't have to be the disciplinarian anymore. He seems to have found a friend in Aled Williams. That's unexpected."

Indeed, Harold was more important than he had ever been when the school was functioning normally. Sir Lionel, obliged to work with him every day as the lawyers, the bank, disgruntled parents, the press, and the police all looked for information.   Harold showed an unexpected coolness under fire. He had, Sir Lionel privately admitted, been seriously under-rated. The departure of DCI Edwards came as a relief, although the financial investigation continued. Harold talked to the remaining police and agreed to provide catering at a modest cost. Mrs Hastings was happy to work on in the school kitchens. The money, she pointed out, would be welcome. She had been left a house which was too large for her. This conversation led to an unexpected consequence as Harold mentioned it one evening to his new friend. Aled Williams decided to register with the County as a supply teacher, ready to teach at any level. It would provide an income as from January. He planned to have more time in which to write a field guide to local birds. He agreed terms with Mrs Hastings to take over part of her house. He would spend most of November packing his belongings.

A temporary replacement was employed as school secretary .Most of the domestic staff left. A handful remained but the interior of the splendid building accumulated dust. The floor no longer gleamed. The windows were not cleaned. As the days grew shorter, the entire building was eerily deserted much of the time and Harold retired to his new accommodation to hear timbers creak, doors slam, windows rattle, but virtually no human sounds once the policemen and women left for the night. He kept his spirits up by planning his escape, once the dreary business was concluded. He would buy a decent campervan and set off to travel round Europe. Meanwhile, he had free accommodation and a decent, guaranteed income. Even after a fair settlement to free himself from Thelma, he would have plenty to carry out his plan. He was, however, also aware that the insurance he and the rest of the staff had paid into had been arranged by Frank Beauchamp. They would have to wait to discover if the money would be available. And that was largely in the hands of the investigating team Harold shrugged, plumped up his pillows and went to sleep.

The Bear had returned to his familiar office in town. He was extremely annoyed to leave the case unsolved, but they had looked into everything. He remained convinced the tampering to Mulcaster's car was the work of Stephen Wilder, but there was no forensic evidence. The case would probably never be solved.
No one blamed The Bear or his team and at least he had been able to pass on the rest of the investigation to DCI Manning.

A call from Manning one day in early October, however, caused him to sit up and listen.

"An ambulance arrived this morning," he was told. "It collected Stephen Wilder. He appears to have overdosed."

"Dead?"

"No. At least I don't think so. He's in your hospital there."

"Right. Thank you."

Rather than telephone the hospital, The Bear drove there. It was less than a mile. Enquiries and the production of a warrant card took him to the ward door. There were two visitors waiting already, Aled Williams and Sir Lionel. They gave him a surprised and hostile stare.

A nurse barred the entrance. "I'm sorry," she said insincerely, "you won't be allowed in for some time. The patient is very ill and receiving treatment."

The Bear flashed his card but got no further.

"Can't you leave the poor man alone, even when he's ill?" Sir Lionel asked, surprising The Bear, who had always seen him as a quiet, unassuming character.

"I have my job to do," said The Bear.

"Everybody has told you Stephen had nothing to do with Mulcaster's accident." It was Aled Williams this time who seemed unusually angry and upset.

"We'll see," said The Bear, and sat down to wait. He was to get no further, however. Stephen Wilder's collapse was the result of years of heavy drinking. Now he suffered all the agonies of withdrawal as well as the physical pain as his liver failed to function. For several days no one was able to see him. When, at last, Sir Lionel was grudgingly allowed to his godson's bedside, he was very shocked. The emaciated, yellow-skinned face was almost unrecognisable. Sunken eyes could not hold their gaze for more than a moment or two. Stephen spoke only in a whisper, brief snatches of conversation which showed he could no longer follow what was said. Sir Lionel touched him lightly and left, profoundly upset.

Stephen Wilder died two days later. The Bear never got to see him.

Chapter thirteen

"What are you going to do with your stuff about bullying?" asked Gordon.

John Shepherd, Beth and Gordon had just eaten a meal which Beth had prepared in her small kitchen.

"Well," said John, "I was planning to produce a series of feature articles on the subject, but Mulcaster's death and his involvement with Greenacres have changed my mind for me."

Gordon and Beth looked at him expectantly.

"I have got interested – distracted, maybe – by the Greenacres business more widely," John explained. "There are so many unanswered questions. I can see the potential for a book instead."

"A book?"

"For the moment I just have to earn a crust by writing short pieces on other subjects, while I spend most of my effort researching the bigger story."

"I take it you are still concentrating on Mulcaster's accident," suggested Gordon, "but now that poor Wilder is dead, can anyone ever prove or disprove it was him that cut the brake pipes?"

"Maybe not," John agreed, "but I've also been looking into aspects of the financial shenanigans."

"That sounds a bit dodgy," said Beth. "DCI Manley may not like you interfering."

John grinned. "I'm sure he won't," he said, "but I can be discreet; I have my own methods and my own sources."

Beth gave him a disapproving look, but he only grinned back. "All part of the fun," he said.

"Surely the police have all kinds of powers at their disposal?" Gordon was curious.

"Of course, they have; access to bank accounts, that sort of thing, but they start by looking at the fraud. I'm starting from a different perspective."

They looked at him, not understanding.

"I wondered," John explained, "just how thoroughly they had looked into Frank Beauchamp's background. His name, by the way, is not Beauchamp, but Beresford."

"How did you find that out?"

"Never ask a journalist to reveal his sources. It's true, and the police know already."

"Go on," said Gordon.

"I'm not sure it's a good idea to say more," said John, hesitating. "I don't want the story to break until I'm ready."

"John! You're not saying we'll have to wait for the book to come out?"

"This is serious, Sis."

"Sorry!"

"If I tell you what I've found out so far, you'll have to swear to keep it to yourselves."

Gordon was now thoroughly intrigued. He and Beth both agreed not to reveal the information.

"Well," said John, settling back with his wine glass refilled, "Frank Beresford had a poor start in life. His mother was the product of a broken home, she was a drunk who probably couldn't have told you who fathered her unwanted baby. The child was rescued by a charity worker in the East End and taken into an orphanage, run by the church. The orphanage was not exactly comfortable or homely. The children were ordered about, made to undertake menial tasks. It was pretty much like the old workhouse.

"Young Frank was obliged to keep his head down just to survive. From what I've discovered so far, there was nothing even resembling kindness, affection or love there. At the age of five he was entered into the local, Church Primary School, where he was taught the three Rs. It was a grim life and Frank continued to survive by being submissive. Then, when he was about eight years old, he had a small piece of good fortune. A new, young teacher arrived. His name was Bugle and he recognised that Frank Beresford had a gift for Arithmetic. Arithmetic was the subject at that time, not Maths. He had to learn the weird and wonderful systems, doing daily sums with pounds, shillings, pence, ha'pennies and farthings, and measurements in yards, rods, chains, furlongs, that sort of thing. "

Neither Beth nor Gordon was entirely sure about all this. They waited for more.

"Mr Bugle must have been pleased to foster the boy's talent. He seems to have given him special tuition and, according to the school logbook, it was Bugle that convinced the Head Teacher to enter Frank for a scholarship offered by a local, private school. He did exceptionally well in the written tests, although his poor appearance and barely articulate speech almost resulted in rejection. At the age of eleven Frank Beresford found himself in a school which challenged his considerable ability. For six months he more than held his own, however, despite being bullied unmercifully by pupils and teachers alike. After all, he was still living in the orphanage.

"The headmaster of the school was –"

"Don't tell us it was Mulcaster!" Gordon exclaimed. "Am I right?"

John nodded. "Bang on," he said, "good old Mulcaster. Not much hope of understanding there, then. But then came a major disaster; Bugle was suffering from TB, and he was taken off to a sanitorium. He never recovered, and he died a year later.

"Frank Beresford struggled on, but remained unpopular, bullied every day. Remarkably, he stuck it out until his fourteenth birthday, when he left and found himself a job in a butcher's shop. His skill with arithmetic was quickly put to use. The butcher was far from good at book-keeping."

"So," asked Beth, "where did it go wrong?",

"It began to go wrong almost straight away," John said. "It might have been otherwise because he managed to enrol for evening classes in book-keeping. He was doing well, but he began fiddling the books to pay the fees. He found it quite easy to deceive his employer, but he grew greedy. He had the job with the butcher for three years until one day the penny dropped, if you'll forgive the joke. The butcher realised his employee was buying new clothes that were more expensive than his modest pay accounted for. He sacked him. Frank was seventeen."

"He wasn't still in the orphanage, surely?" Beth asked. "Where was he living?"

"That was obviously another problem. He had lodgings but now he had no money, but this was 1939, just before war broke out. He joined the army, saying he was eighteen.

"In the army, sad to say, he soon realised there were more opportunities to make money. His studies paid off and he was soon in the Pay Corps. He had learned from his experience with the butcher, not to be so greedy that it would draw attention, so he became skilled as a thief."

"And he got away with it?"

"Until 1944, yes. He was chucked out then. For a couple of years, he associated with a gang of petty criminals in London. He was arrested and spent six months in jail. It was then that he changed his name and, when he was discharged, got himself a job in the insurance company you probably know about. He forged the references. He met Irma and they moved in together. I'm not sure how much Irma was told about his past."

"Wow!" said Gordon, "That's some story! How on earth did you find all that out?"

"Remember," John said, "don't tell anyone any of this."

"You said," Beth spoke quietly, "that Frank Beresford was bullied at school."

"Continuously and unmercifully," John confirmed.

"And the headmaster was Mulcaster?"

Her brother nodded, looking in her eyes. The implications had reached the two listeners. Frank Beresford had been driven out of the school which might have provided an education to save him. He had learned how to be a petty criminal. He had acquired a police record, associated with other criminals, and ended up in a position where he could steal money almost at will. Then along came Mulcaster, a man he must have detested for twenty years, and a man with similar, even superior skills in accountancy. It would have been a matter of weeks, perhaps days, before Mulcaster spotted the irregularities which Frank had introduced. After all this time Mulcaster would not identify Frank Beauchamp with a former pupil, but he would assuredly sniff out false record-keeping.

"You say you're not sure how much of all this Irma knew about?"

"No."

"The spare keys to the workshop were looked after by Irma," Gordon pointed out.

"Yes, it's not clear if she was in on the sabotage."

They sat for a while and thought over what John had told them

"Shouldn't you tell all this to DCI Manley?" Beth was clearly worried.

"No." Her brother was emphatic. "All of this is information the police could discover for themselves. They may have it already. It's all circumstantial. I'm not ready to do their work for them, either. I don't know DCI Manley and I am not eager to help DCI Blundell. I didn't much like the man. Don't forget your promise to remain quiet about this."

There was another silence as Gordon and Beth considered this.

"OK," Gordon said at last. "It is circumstantial, you're right, but if you dig up hard evidence, you'll have to pass it on, surely?"

"It would be an offence not to, though there might be room for debate about what is meant by hard evidence."

They left it at that. The subject turned to Beth's new job. She was looking forward to teaching more theory and had already begun to brush up her knowledge of nutrition and especially the digestive process.

In his familiar office The Bear received a telephone call from DCI Manley.

"Ted," Manley began, "the Beauchamps or Beresfords are at each other's throats. I was interviewing Frank this morning, when he threw a dirty great spanner in the works."

"What kind of spanner?"

"I was trying to establish how deeply his wife was implicated in the book-keeping fraud," said Manley. "She has been claiming she knew nothing about the embezzlement until he forced her to leave with him in their old van."

"She must have known."

"She says not."

The Bear grunted. "She's as guilty as he is."

"More so, according to her husband. Whatever their relationship was before they ran off, it has changed into open warfare now. I suspect they are both lying through their teeth."

"What's happened exactly?"

"Frank Beresford claims it was Irma who tampered with the brakes on Mulcaster's car."

"Irma? Why?"

"They had both been told Mulcaster was a qualified accountant, and they knew he would soon uncover the false accounting."

"Well." The Bear agreed, "it would give either of them a motive. But why Irma?"

"There remains the uncertainty about getting rid of the drained oil."

"Yes?"

"Frank swears it was Irma who did it. He points out she had direct access to the spare workshop keys. He didn't see her take them out of the cupboard, but he say he saw her putting them back on their hook the next morning."

"He had the same access."

"Irma denies it, as you'd expect. She's spitting fury, says it was Frank."

"Good to hear they are fighting."

"Eh?"

"When they are fighting, they are most likely to contradict themselves and each other."

"Never thought of it like that. What do you want to do about it?"

"I'll have another go at Irma, shake her up a bit further. She's a cool customer, though. After that, I'll have another go with Frank. He's a professional liar, of course. He's also technically your prisoner at the moment."

"Be my guest. Could this be the breakthrough you need?"

"I shouldn't think so. It certainly suggests we can forget about the other suspects for the time being/"

"Wilder, you mean"

"He was certainly the front runner until he died."

"Who's the other?"

"The mechanic, Jackson. He has the only other set of keys."

"Well, good luck with your questions."

"Thanks, but if one or other of the Beauchamps – sorry, Beresfords – is guilty, without hard evidence, we may never know."

Irma Beresford sat on the other side of the table, her face set in an icy expression. A solicitor she had requested sat beside her. They faced The Bear and Sergeant Rawlings, who inserted twin tapes into the recorder. They waited until the recorder was ready. Rawlings announced who was present.

"Mrs Beauchamp," The Bear began.

"Beresford," the solicitor interrupted.

"Right, Mrs Beresford, you accuse your husband of tampering with the brakes on Mr Mulcaster's car?"

"Yes."

"That action, as you are aware, led directly to the fatal accident the following morning."

"Yes."

"You were, you say, aware that your husband was responsible."

"Yes."

"Yet you failed to report this fact to the police."

"No."

"Why not, since that failure makes you guilty as an accomplice?"

"Frank was my husband. And I was afraid of him."

"Afraid of him?" This was a new element. The Bear could not readily believe Irma Beresford would ever be afraid of anyone, least of all her seemingly meek husband.

"Afraid of him?"

"You wouldn't understand," said Irma. "When I met Frank and got to know him, he managed somehow to take over my mind."

"What on earth are you talking about?"

"Inspector," the female solicitor interrupted. "Frank Beresford was what is known as a control freak. You may not have come across the kind of husbands like him. Soon after they married, she found herself trapped. He wouldn't let her out of his sight, watched her every move. She was cut off from her friends…"

"Let her speak for herself," said The Bear, thinking this was a load of complete nonsense. To Irma he said, "If you were entirely innocent in all this, the false accounting as well as the damage to the car, why did you agree to leave with your husband?"

"For the same reason," Irma replied. "I couldn't get away from him. If I'd tried, he would have followed and taken me back by force."

The interview was taking an unexpected direction. The Bear was beginning to feel he was losing control.

"Let me get back to some concrete facts," he said. "Your husband states that he saw you replacing the keys to the workshop on the morning of the crash."

"He's lying."

"These were the only keys, other than those held by Jackson?"

"Yes, but I never took them from the cupboard."

"Did you see your husband take them or even replace them?"

Irma hesitated, frowning. "No," she said, "I never actually saw him, but the office was locked whenever I was not there."

"You say he never let you out of his sight," said The Bear. "What about when I asked you into my office?"

"The intercom system was always left turned on."

This came as an unpleasant surprise. It meant Frank Beresford could have eavesdropped on all The Bear's conversations and interviews. He felt anger begin to creep up on him.

"It seems to me," he said, "the two of you are a pair of conniving crooks."

"Chief Inspector!" The solicitor began to protest.

"This interview is over," said The Bear. Rawlings turned off the machine. One of the tapes was handed to the lawyer. The meeting had produced nothing of value.

Frank Beresford stuck to his story; he had witnessed Irma replacing the keys in the cupboard on the morning of the accident. She had even admitted to him, he said, that she had used the keys the previous evening to collect a pair of tinsnips. She had seen the metal tray and realised it would conceal the damage if she took away the brake fluid back to the workshop. Jackson was always out on Monday evenings.

There were obvious inconsistencies between the two accounts. If Frank Beresford exerted a Svengali-like influence over his wife, and kept he under constant observation, she could not have carried out the crime without his seeing her.

There was insufficient evidence either way. DCI Manley had uncovered enough in his investigation to warrant charges of fraud. Fraud investigations were notoriously long-drawn-out, however. Irma Beresford was required to hold herself ready for further questioning, both in respect of the fraud and possibly into the damage to the car. Meanwhile, since no charges had been brought, she was suspended from her secretarial post, but allowed to stay on in the Steward's House.

October brought several weeks of autumnal sunshine before the sky clouded over and an easterly wind brought leaves swirling from the trees. Then came a week of rain. The grass on either side of the school buildings was no longer dry enough to cut. The tractor was stored in the shed. The big doors were locked. Beth was away for a week at her new job, looking for somewhere to live in January. Gordon continued his exercising after every morning run, from which he returned, soaked to the skin, with even his trainers squelching. But the regime was paying dividends. He had never been fitter.

When he made his way each day to the school gym, ignoring the dustiness of unpolished floors and prepared to clean the showers for himself, he was more and more conscious of the echoing hollowness of the building. By now only a handful of residents remained. The gardener had been retained, though Gordon did not know why. At least the Gardener's House, which he shared, felt a little less empty.

He did not want to spend too much money, so did not go out much, but he took an occasional trip to the cinema. Except for the week when she was away, Gordon continued to run with Beth, but she planned to spend Christmas with her family.

There was some activity still going on. DCI Masley and his team remained at the school. Mrs Hastings continued to prepare meals for them, and she often provided Gordon with the odd snack. Harold Black was always present. Sir Lionel was frequently to be seen, working with Harold much of the time. A steady stream of other people came to help determine the fate of Greenacres. There was work for a whole group of assorted lawyers and accountants. Watching the comings and goings, Gordon felt vague distaste to see these well-dressed professionals in their smart suits picking over the bones, like vultures cleaning up the carcase of a once-beautiful antelope.

Halfway through November Beth invited him to a farewell meal. She would be leaving the following day. They remained comfortable with one another, at ease, but this meal would be the last for a long time, and the last in this flat. The occasion was tinged with sadness as a result. Beth, on the other hand, remained excited at the prospect of a new, demanding job. The money from the sale of her grandmother's cottage meant she was able to begin negotiations for the purchase of a small house not too far from the university. Prices, she reported, were much lower in the north.

"You're off to Somerset soon, I suppose," she observed.

"Yes. Ten days."

"Enjoy your bedmaking."

"Thanks."

"You'll certainly be fit for it," she commented. "Will you be able to work out at this new place?"

"Yes. There's a well-equipped gymnasium as well as a lot of sporting facilities. There's even a nine-hole golf course, a swimming pool, archery, that sort of thing. You can go riding, if you like. I don't know how much time I'll have for all that sort of thing, mind you."

Beth laughed. "Sounds just the thing for you," she said. "Any idea what to do after that?"

"Yes," Gordon replied. Something in his expression held her attention. "It's a major reason I've been in training for the past month."

She looked at him, waiting.

"I'm joining the army," he announced.

"The army?"

"Once the idea came to me, I grew to like it more and more. I've been into the recruitment office and found out a lot. I shall aim to become a PE Instructor."

"Wow!" Beth said nothing more for a while as she thought over what he said. "You may have to kill people," she said.

Gordon laughed. "It's possible, I suppose, but not all that probable. If I can get into the right line of work, I'll not only be helping other people get fitter, but I'm also sure there will be opportunities to take part in sports."

"Well," she replied, "I must say it's a surprise, but I suppose it has its good side."

"I think so. I won't have to worry about accommodation. I shall be fed well. The first month or two may be hard, but I'm now pretty fit. I should be ready to deal with the physical training."

"How definite is it you'll get into the PE training?"

"Nothing's certain," Gordon admitted. "A lot will probably depend on how well I get on in the first few weeks."

"And do you think you're ready to submit to discipline?"

"I think so. I've certainly given it some thought. I know I'll have to accept the discipline."

"I wish you luck," said Beth. "I don't think I'd like it, but if it's what you want..."

"My mind is made up. I think the army will provide a lot of opportunities for travel, as well, I hope as experience in the field of PE. When I finish, at the very least I shall be well qualified for work as a civilian in something like a sports centre or a gymnasium. I may, with any luck, have broken into the professional sports teams. The army produces good athletes. Some even get to perform in the Olympics."

"It's good to see you so enthusiastic," Beth observed. "I hope you won't forget me. Keep in touch. I'll want to know how it works out."

Neither of them wanted to allow the friendship to end. Both were about to set off on a new phase in their lives, both would be challenged.

Chapter fourteen

"The usual, please Fred," Rawlings said.

"Let me get this." Rawlings turned to look at the man who spoke. "You don't know me," the man said.

"Oh, yes, I do," said Rawlings. "You're John Shepherd, journalist. You came to Greenacres School last year, when we were investigating the death of the headmaster."

"I'm surprised you remember me."

"It's what we're trained to do. But I'll buy my own drinks, thank you. I'd never let a reporter buy me anything. It could so easily be misconstrued."

"Suit yourself. I was going to do you a favour, not ask you for one."

Rawlings carried his pint to an empty table. Shepherd followed him. They both sat, Rawlings watching the other man warily.

"I got very interested in the Greenacres business," Shepherd began.

"I can't tell you anything about it,"Rawlings said. "Don't even try."

"I don't want to ask you anything," Shepherd insisted. "Far from it. I want to give you some information, or, at least, some ideas."

"I'm not even concerned with the Greenacres business any longer," Rawlings said, impatient to be left in peace.

"It is quite a while ago," Shepherd said. "What you don't know is that I have been writing a book about the whole affair. The publishers are keen to bring it out, but they're waiting for the fraud case to be heard."

"I have just said I am not involved in the ongoing enquiries. I cannot and will not talk to you about it."

John Shepherd smiled and spread his hands as an indication of his innocent intent.

"I realise that," he said. "I told you, I want to give you something, not ask for information."

Rawlings looked even more suspicious.

"I told you I've been writing a book about the entire business. No one has ever been charged with the damage to Mulcaster's car."

"No."

"You don't need to confirm or deny this, but I understand there was no forensic evidence to suggest who cut the brake pipes on the car, causing it to crash and so killing Mulcaster."

Rawlings, as suggested, did not comment.

"Now," said Shepherd, warming to his task, "it has been assumed that the person who cut those pipes came prepared with the wherewithal to collect the brake fluid, and the most convenient place to get it was in the nearby workshop. It seems a reasonable plan. The problem is that the workshop was locked. The teacher who ran the workshop, Jackson, had a set of keys, but he was off the school premises all night. The only other set of keys was kept in the school office. The school secretary and her husband, the Bursar, both had access to the keys."

Rawlings said nothing but was listening closely.

"Don't ask me where I got the information," said Shepherd. "It doesn't matter. I believe that neither of the Beresfords, or Beauchamps, as they were then calling themselves, has admitted using the keys, but that Frank Beresford has said he saw his wife returning the keys to the office on the morning of the accident. It's a case of a proven liar's word against that of his wife."

Still Rawlings was silent.

"Now, here's the thing," said Shepherd. "What if neither of them used the keys? The place where the car was parked was almost as close to the Steward's House as it was to the workshop.

Rawlings replied. "The forensic team dis a thorough search of the Steward's House," he said. "There were no traces of anything there."

"I took that as read," said Shepherd. "What about their garage or car port?"

"That, too."

"Now, I'll say again, don't ask where I got the information, but, when the Beresfords were caught and brought back to the school, did anyone search their van?"

"Of course. They had taken incriminating documents with them."

"But did anyone think to check the toolbox?"

Rawlings was staring at Shepherd.

"I have found out," said the journalist, that the team who searched the van listed everything.

They were meticulous. The toolbox was well equipped to maintain the vehicle. Among other items, it contained a sharp pair of pliers, capable of cutting cables or brake pipes. It also contained a large, white enamel pudding tin. There was also a mall funnel and a plastic bottle. The attack on the car could have been made without access to the workshop."

"Assuming you have the facts right," said Rawlings after a while, "it doesn't take us any further. It could still be either of them."

Shepherd shrugged. "I imagine DCI Blundell would be interested in the theory," he said.

"It's not hard evidence, though."

"No. The Chief Inspector and I were not exactly on good terms, which is why I told you about this. He would probably listen if you told him."

"So, you do want something from me!"

"Not really. I've given you my idea. What you do with it is up to you." He finished his pint, stood up and nodded goodbye.

Rawlings watched him go. He was both impressed and annoyed at the detailed information Shepherd had obtained. It was accurate, and someone in the force, probably in forensics, must have leaked the facts. He was also annoyed because he knew he would have to tell his boss about the encounter with Shepherd. It was likely to be a bad-tempered affair and for no good reason. Shepherd had not produced any hard, useable evidence. It was probable that the brake pipes had been cut by one or other of the Beresfords, but it remained uncertain which one. He drained his glass and went to the bar for another pint.

"Shepherd! He has still been poking about, has he? I take it you didn't tell him anything?"

"No, Boss, you know me better than that."

"Well, someone has been talking."

"It sounds like someone on the team that examined the van."

"Yes, it does."

"His theory might be right," Rawlings admitted, "but it doesn't even narrow down the choice between them."

"It might."

"How?"

"The husband swears he saw his wife return the workshop keys. He accuses her directly of cutting the brakes."

"Yes?"

"In other words, he is saying the tinsnips and other stuff came from the workshop."

"Yes?"

"If Shepherd is right, then Beresford could simply be lying through his teeth again, He knows we thought the stuff used came from the workshop, so he played along with that to mislead us. His wife has never suggested any other means were used."

"No?"

"Unless he admits to tampering with the car, we shall never be sure. We could never make the accusation stick."

Rawlings watched and waited.

"I hate this bloody case!" The Bear exclaimed. "It started as an enquiry into a suspicious death. We got as far as establishing the cause, but we never have been able to charge either Frank or Irma Beresford. I hate not having a definite answer. Meanwhile, Manley takes over the rest of the case. I imagine he will end up with a successful prosecution for fraud. We've had to walk away with only a failure."

He was still sore, Rawlings could see.

"I think we should pay Mr Beresford one more visit," said The Bear. "We shan't ever have sufficient evidence to charge him, but at least we can get him to show it wasn't his wife."

"I hope," said The Bear sarcastically, "you are comfortable here.

Frank Beresford looked round at the plain, grey walls of the prison room, then at the two visitors. "Can't complain," he said. He looked uneasy, unsure why DCI Blundell and Sergeant Rawlings were back, talking to him. He had spent many hours with DCI Manley and several other policemen, as they delved into the intricate, financial system he had set up. He had implicated many others. Now, he could only wait until the trial was brought to court. He would probably remain here on remand for the best part of another year. He would have preferred to be in Spain, in the villa he had ready for him, but for the moment he must remain where he was.

"Mr Beresford," The Bear said at last, "I want you to tell us once more why you accused your wife of cutting the brakes on Granville Mulcaster's car."

"I've told you all about it."

"Let me get it straight," The Bear said. "You say you saw your wife returning the workshop keys on the morning of the accident,"

"Right."

"Didn't you ask her why she had them?"

Beresford looked from one to the other. "Not at the time, no," he said.

"Not at the time? You have never told us you talked to her about this."

"It was later on," said Beresford. "When it was clear the brakes had been tampered with."

"Why would your wife have done that?"

"The stupid bitch said she was trying to protect me."

"Protect you?"

"She knew I had been cooking the books, and she knew this Mulcaster chap was a trained accountant. She said she wanted to scare him off."

"You didn't tell us this before."

"We had a serious row," Beresford said. "I told her she had made everything much worse. I knew your lot would get involved and God knew what they would start digging up. We had to get away in the end."

"She told you how she took the tools from the workshop?"

"Yes."

"How good was your wife at looking after your vehicle?"

"Eh! Why do you ask? She knew enough to cut the brake pipes," Beresford said. "She wasn't much of a mechanic. I'd never let her loose on our campervan."

"You looked after that yourself, then?"

"Yes. And don't say anything about the broken back axle. That's not the kind of problem you could predict. I looked after that van really well. I would never have let Irma touch it, though she did drive it sometimes."

"One last thing," said The Bear, "you say your wife was responsible for the damage to the car?"

"Yes."

"She told you she had used the keys to the workshop in order to find tinsnips and get rid of the brake fluid?"

"That's right."

"What if I were to tell you the drainage tray left an impression in the grass?"

"And?"

"And that impression was a good deal smaller than the tray in the workshop."

"You'll have to ask her about that. I don't know what the tray looked like."

"How much brake fluid would you say there would be in the system?"

Beresford was beginning to look less certain.

"Something under a pint," he said.

"Enough to fill a modest pudding basin?"

Beresford did not reply. He stared at the two men opposite, his lips tightly shut, then he said,

"You're trying to fit me up! I've told you; it was that hard-nosed bitch I married. You don't have any evidence. You can't have."

"I think we know the truth," The Bear said. He stood up and called for the prison officer to let them out.

"He's right, Boss," Rawlings said as they headed for the car park. "We still have no hard evidence."

"No, but I'm sure he did it."

Rawlings slid into the passenger seat and lit a cigarette. "I don't remember all that about marks in the grass where the dish was," he said.

The Bear, reaching forward to put the key in the ignition, gave one of his rare smiles. "I,made that up," he said.

Rawlings said nothing but grinned in his turn. They both knew Beresford could never be charged with the crime. He would escape the charge of manslaughter. The worst thing that would happen to him would be a spell in prison, convicted of fraud. The time he had already spent on remand would be taken off. He would get off far too lightly. The only consolation for

The Bear was the knowledge that he was sure he knew the truth. Sometimes, you have to let these things go.

Publication of John Shepherd's book was delayed as the lawyers examined all the legal implications for the various people mentioned in the text. The school governors came out of the affair none too well. Mulcaster, the pivotal character in the narrative, was revealed as a bully whose success was based on very unpleasant dealings with staff and pupils. The publishers hesitated still further, fearing that sales would be affected by the perception of a biased author, destroying the reputation of the dead man. When, eventually, the book was published, it proved very controversial, and it sparked off a heated debate, not about bullying, the author's intention, but about the very existence of fee-paying, private schools.

Greenacres was at last sold to a consortium of investors. The buildings were modified until only the main façade remained as it was in 1890. The grounds were landscaped to provide a golf course. Gordon was now a corporal, a PE Instructor, exploring many sporting opportunities in his chosen career. Greenacres' new function as a residential sports centre would have delighted him, but it was well beyond anything he could afford.

Harold Black, motoring round the south of France and Italy, was happier than he thought possible, as he wrote to Aled Williams.

The new Comprehensive School benefitted greatly from the closure of Greenacres. Within three years plans were afoot to enlarge and develop it further.

The Bear, following all these changes in the local newspaper, was content deling with a steady stream of petty crimes. He attended the Crown Court for Beresford's trial. He grunted at the guilty verdict, was disappointed at the sentence – eight years meant that, given the time already served, Beresford would be free in a year. DCI Manley had long since returned to London. The Bear was due to retire within two years. He had no idea what he would do.

Irma Beresford was not charged with any crime or offence. She was taken back as secretary by Sir Lionel for a further year, then left. She changed her name, hoping her former husband would not track her down. In fact, he did not do so, heading as soon as he could for Spain.

Sergeant Rawlings stopped his car at the side of the road to look at the beautifully painted sign. "Greenacres Country Club and Golf Course" he read. Underneath was a telephone number. The place would probably flourish. He understood the high prices were justified by the quality of the service. They had employed a Michelin star chef. But Rawlings was thinking philosophically. The Greenacres affair was like a large rock thrown into a placid pool. For a short time, the waves and ripples washed against the shores. Now the last ripples had subsided, and the waters were calm, even beautiful. A newcomer would never know there had been a disturbance.

He turned the key in the ignition, glanced in his mirror, and began the short drive home.

THE END

Lightning Source UK Ltd.
Milton Keynes UK
UKHW011354020822
406731UK00002B/607